Adrienne

Adrienne

Judy
Baer

BETHANY HOUSE PUBLISHERS
MINNEAPOLIS, MINNESOTA 55438
A Division of Bethany Fellowship, Inc.

Adrienne
Judy Baer

Library of Congress Catalog Card Number 87-71605

ISBN 0–87123–949–3

Published by Bethany House Publishers
A Division of Bethany Fellowship, Inc.
6820 Auto Club Road, Minneapolis, Minnesota 55438

Printed in the United States of America

To my daughter,
Adrienne Fosen Baer,
With love.

JUDY BAER received a B.A. in English and Education from Concordia College in Moorhead, Minnesota. She has had eight novels published and is a member of the national Romance Writers of America and the National Federation of Press Women. She is married, the mother of two children and their home is in Cando, North Dakota.

Chapter One

"The hunters have moved into the cabin."

Adrienne Fuller's eyebrow arched in surprise at her father's statement. Was it that time of year already?

"It's hard to believe hunting season is about to begin. Where *did* the summer go?" Her mother shook her head in disbelief.

Adrienne groaned, stretching her arms high over her head with a boneless, cat-like grace. Her bottom lip came out in a disgusted pout. "I think somebody cancelled summer."

Wayne Fuller chuckled. "Quit moping, Adrienne. Just 'cause you have to sit in school a few hours a day doesn't mean it's the end of the world."

Mr. and Mrs. Fuller both hid twitching grins from their daughter. Bridling Adrienne and sending her off to school was a bit like harnessing moonbeams—difficult to impossible.

"I thought you said you *liked* school this year."

"It's better," Adrienne acknowledged grudgingly, flipping her auburn bangs away from her eyes. "Better classes. Lots of science and math. And science labs. I hope we get to do *tons* of experiments." Her dark eyes brightened with anticipation.

"Pray for the Hartwell School District, Naomi. They're in big trouble now." Mr. Fuller almost kept a smile off his face.

Adrienne rolled her eyes in mock despair. Parents. They never quite understood. What was so special about school when there was *life* to be lived? She flipped her red pageboy away from her shoulders. Her brown eyes danced with excitement.

"Maybe we can dissect sharks instead of frogs this semester. That would be fun."

"Uproarious fun, I'm sure."

"Well, it *would* be. How am I ever going to be a doctor if I don't do these things?"

"And how are you going to be a doctor if you don't want to go to school?"

"Well," Adrienne wrinkled her freckled-spattered nose, "it's just so *boring* sometimes."

"*My* life hasn't been boring since the day you were born," Naomi Fuller admonished. "I've had lizards in the bathtub, snakes in the kitchen sink and unidentifiable remains of things I don't want to consider in the newly washed pockets of your clothes ever since you were old enough to toddle. Being within ten feet of you makes life exciting, Adrienne. Trust me. I should know."

Naomi's eyes grazed the pert profile of her only daughter. Adrienne was dressed in faded denim and lavender today, body skimming jeans and a baggy, knee-length sweatshirt. She smelled of something part flowers, part musk and a hint of rubbing alcohol. No doubt it had been concocted from a chemistry kit and the blooms she had picked in the yard.

"Enough about school, already," Wayne interjected.

Wisely, Adrienne turned to her plate. Through a mouthful of pancakes, she inquired, "Are the same hunters at the cabin this year as last? Mr. Sandshill and his friends?"

The cabin was a compact log house nestled in the woods at the far reaches of the Fuller property. Grandpa Fuller had built it as a retreat for his wife who loved to paint the flora and fauna of the lush Minnesota landscape. Now it had become a yearly gathering place for city hunters who wanted a week or a month in the wilds to "rough it" before going back to Minneapolis with their tales of adventures in the north woods.

"No. Sandshill couldn't make it this year. It's the fellow who answered my ad in the Minneapolis paper." Wayne sloshed more milk into his glass.

"Just one person? Won't that be lonely?"

"It's a family, I believe. The man said he had his sons with him. I'll have to mosey up there today and see how they're getting settled."

"Are they staying long?"

" 'Indefinite,' the fellow said. He asked about staying through deer season. That doesn't begin for some time yet. Seems funny he'd want to stay that long, but it's none of my business. Just so they pay the rent."

"Don't his kids have to go to school?" Adrienne inquired. The curiosity in her eyes was hooded beneath dark, spikey lashes that tilted upward at the tips.

"Seems this man must have been a teacher at one time. Said he was tutoring the older boy at home. Guess it doesn't matter where they stay then."

"Lucky dog."

"Adrienne . . ." her parents warned together.

Reluctantly, Adrienne focused her attention on the milk carton in front of her, deciding it was wise not to attract any more of her parents' attention.

Calories, fortified with vitamin D, calcium. . . . She surveyed the carton disinterestedly. With her index finger she poked the waxed box until the other side came into view.

A little hiss of dismay whispered through her pursed lips. This was one of those dreadful cartons with pictures of missing children stamped into the cardboard and wax. The words *Have you seen this child?* blared across the expanse. Quickly she pushed the carton aside.

She didn't like those ads. Or the ones that came on the television news either. She didn't like to be reminded that there were children who weren't home—safe with their parents and families, that there were children who had been spirited away from those they loved. And she didn't want to imagine what might have happened to them. Her imagination was too vivid, too intense for that.

"Something wrong, Adrienne?" her father inquired.

"Nah. Just those dumb milk cartons."

"The pictures on them?"

"Yeh. They give me the creeps."

Wayne's eyes glowed with understanding. "Under that tough exterior beats the heart of a marshmallow, right, Adrienne?"

She glared at her father from beneath the red, spikey points of her bangs. Then the glare softened. "Right, Daddy."

Silently, Adrienne and her dad found each other's fingers across the top of the table. She could feel the thick calluses and work-roughened skin beneath her palms. Her father gave her hand a gentle squeeze.

Silently, Adrienne gave a word of thanks for what she so often took for granted. Blessed by God. That's what she was. It was an old-fashioned word, one she only heard in church. But it was the word that described her life. Blessed.

Before either of her parents could guess at her sentimentality, she pushed away from the table. "Gotta go. Bus will be here in a minute."

Her father nodded.

"Here's your school bag, Adrienne." Naomi bustled from the pantry. "Tonight you can help me hang fresh curtains in the cabin. Your dad is going to stock the firewood. Then our hunters will be all set."

"And you can meet those boys. . . ." Wayne interjected.

A pinprick of curiosity needled her. "How old did you say the boys were?"

Wayne chuckled aloud. "Is either boy fifteen or older? Is that what you *really* mean?"

"Daddy!"

"I'd say the eldest is about your age, Adrienne. Nice looking kid, too. You might want to begin stocking the firewood up there yourself. What do you think?" he teased.

"Very funny," she retorted. "I'm not interested enough in boys to do manual labor just to look at them."

"Good! Glad to hear it!" Wayne threw an arm about his daughter and they strolled toward the front door. The bus was pulling into the yard as the screen door shuddered shut behind her.

Jill Wainright had a seat saved for her at the back of the bus.

"Here, Adrienne! Back here!" Jill waved both arms and screeched over the cacophony of voices. Her braces glinted in the sunlight and her fine blonde hair spun like a halo around her head.

"Hi! How'd you get the back seat? It's usually taken." Adrienne threw herself full force into the stiff leather bench.

Jill's nose wrinkled. "The Brain got to drive to school today. I saw him in his dad's car."

"Well, at least he couldn't grab the back seat that way."

"He just likes it back here 'cause he doesn't have

to talk to anyone. He can stick his nose in a book and pretend we're all invisible."

"Maybe we are," Adrienne murmured thoughtfully.

"Maybe we are what?" Jill puzzled.

"Invisible. To him, at least. Maybe it would help if we painted chemical formulas or algebraic equations on our foreheads."

"Well," Jill pouted, "I don't like it. You're smart and you aren't stuck up."

Adrienne shrugged. She didn't feel like worrying about Kyle "The Brain" Rogers today. Nothing was ever going to get his nose out of a book anyway.

"I thought you were going to call me last night," Jill accused, glaring over the stack of books on her lap.

"Couldn't. Mom had me washing and ironing stuff for the cabin. Just in time too. Dad said at breakfast the hunters have already moved in."

"I can't see why it is so much fun to spend your vacation roughing it in a little log cabin when there are perfectly nice Holiday Inns all over the country."

"It's the hunting, Jill. Ducks, geese, deer—you know. Best hunting in the world, my dad says. And it's pretty and peaceful up at the cabin."

"And good extra income that goes into your college account," Jill added knowingly.

"Doesn't hurt," Adrienne grinned. She wanted more than anything to be a doctor. And every day someone rented that cabin put her closer to her goal.

That had been the deal. If she helped with the cabin chores, the rental money would go into a college savings program. She hoped these new people stayed a long time.

The thought of medical school prodded her memory. She turned to Jill. "Did you get the proposal for our science display ready?" She and Jill had been the only sophomores chosen to set up the biology room display during the junior/senior fall science fair. It was a feather in her cap, Adrienne thought. Maybe one of the judges from the university would take notice while they were here to judge the older students' work.

Jill's mobile face crumpled. "No. I looked through all sorts of books and thought and thought, but I can't come up with anything. You're so smart, Adrienne. Why don't you come up with an idea?"

Adrienne scooted down in the seat and braced her knees against the seat in front of her. "I can't think either. It has to be special. It has to be the best science display Hartwell's biology department has ever had.

"I don't understand why you care so much, Adrienne."

"Don't you see?" Adrienne swiveled to face her friend. "If we do something interesting, maybe one of the senior division judges will notice. Everything helps when you're trying to get into med school!"

"You're only fifteen, Adrienne," Jill reminded her friend. "It's not like your bags are already packed."

"But I don't want to make any mistakes. My folks haven't got enough money to put me through all those years. If I do well now, maybe I can earn a scholarship."

"And maybe you and The Brain should be doing a project together. He's probably going to put a satellite into orbit or genetically create some new organism. . . ."

"Yeh," Adrienne pondered.

"Hey! I wasn't serious!" Jill yelped, seeing the expression on her friend's face.

Adrienne sighed. "It's a dumb idea. Kyle Rogers is too boring to do a project with," she paused and stared out the window, "and anyway, he'd never ask me. He's so serious."

"And he uses all those big words."

"And he doesn't know we exist, anyway."

" 'Cause he's two years older and thinks he's smart."

"He *is* smart, Jill," Adrienne reminded her friend.

"Yeh, but he doesn't have to *think* it."

"Maybe he's just shy."

"Shy? Kyle? What do *you* know about 'shy,' Adrienne?" Jill prodded. "You haven't been shy a day in your life!"

Thoughtfully Adrienne tapped her toe against the steel frame of the seat. "Maybe you don't know me as well as you thought, Jill."

Jill's eyes widened. "Really?"

"Maybe some people hide shyness behind jokes and crazy clothes and clowning around."

Jill nodded, looking at Adrienne with round eyes. "Maybe you're right."

Two quiet girls made their way off the Hartwell bus, but their contemplative mood was quickly shattered by a riot in the halls near the science lab.

"Catch it! Catch it!"

"Where'd it go? Did you see where it went?"

"Under there."

"That's the toe of my boot, stupid!"

"Find him before he gets hurt."

"Becky Overlund fainted. Should we pick her up?"

"You can't leave her lying there!"

"Find it!"

"Quiet!" The last scream came from Mr. Palley, the science instructor. Adrienne had never seen him so pale and grim looking.

"Some prankster who, if I ever catch him, is going to spend the rest of his high school career washing blackboards, has thought it humorous to release the boa constrictor from its enclosure. It is imperative that we find Melvin before he locates an air duct and disappears into the walls of this school forever. I need volunteers to help me look."

From the corner of her eye, Adrienne noticed Rory Olson and Mike Wills trying vainly to suppress their laughter. She grimaced. Rory Olson was a jerk. He thought losing Melvin was a big joke.

Mr. Palley glanced grimly to the prone figure of a girl on the floor. "And will someone please help Miss Overlund to the school infirmary?"

"She's not sick. She's just scared of snakes!" someone piped from the back.

"Be that as it may, I want her in the infirmary. And I want those of you *not* scared of snakes to assist me in the search."

It was odd, Adrienne thought later, what happened next. The crowd of milling students seemed to melt backward, away from Mr. Palley and toward the outer periphery of the hall until only she and Kyle Rogers and a handful of other boys were left standing alone in a semi-circle of students.

"No others want to search?" Mr. Palley inquired.

Melvin hadn't been a popular snake.

His eating habits had offended ninety-nine percent of the female class members when they watched a rather large rat with an amazingly long tail go down Melvin's throat both whole and live.

As if that weren't enough, Melvin had wrapped himself around one of the senior boys who hadn't had instructions in handling and squeezed too tightly. Seeing Hartwell High's star football player having difficulty extricating himself from Melvin's caress had alienated even more of Melvin's supporters. The tiny group waited for instructions.

"Very well, then. We must move quickly. He can get through any opening larger than this." Mr. Palley made a circle with his fingers to indicate Melvin's size and started down the corridor.

Adrienne, Kyle and the others hurried to keep up.

As the search party crawled on their hands and knees, peeking under the recesses, shelves and lockers for the missing snake, more than once Adrienne found herself shoulder to shoulder with Kyle. Soon, they were smiling each time their arms or heads or legs bumped one another as they searched the far recesses of the school building.

Melvin was finally located at lunchtime. He'd attempted to take up residence in the dark, safe tunnel under the bleachers in the gymnasium where the odors of stale popcorn and dirty sneakers mingled.

Adrienne dusted off the knees of her jeans. "Yuk! I didn't know that this school had so many creepy, out-of-the-way places."

Kyle grinned. It was a nice grin, exceptionally so. It brightened and warmed his blue eyes. The thought flashed through Adrienne's mind that it was too bad he so often kept it hidden.

He was silent for a moment, but Adrienne never minded silence. It was much better than silly, idle chatter.

"You're a good sport, you know."

Adrienne's dark eyes flew open in surprise. "Me?" The word came out in a squeak, much like the lately departed science lab rat.

"You. I didn't see any other girls grubbing around looking for Melvin."

"If he'd gotten in the heat ducts, he could have popped in and out of every classroom in the school and terrorized everybody for weeks."

"True. But not many volunteered to help."

"It was nothing." Adrienne shrugged, wishing that she'd worn her new flowered sweatshirt instead of the plain lavender one.

"You're very self-effacing."

"Huh?" Adrienne looked up quickly.

"You, know—self-abnegating."

"What?"

"Modest! You're modest!"

"Then why didn't you say that the first time?"

"I did. You just didn't understand me."

"Then you'd better learn to speak our language." She felt a pinprick of irritation until she noticed Kyle's face.

"I know. I do it all the time. I scare people off with my vocabulary. I'm sorry." He looked truly miserable.

"Don't be sorry. You're just too smart for the rest of us. Come down to our level, that's all." For a moment, Adrienne actually felt sorry for him. *Too smart.* She hadn't thought anyone could be that. But maybe it was possible—if it separated a person from people who would otherwise be his friends.

The blank, distant gaze that Kyle usually wore was back in place. The warmth in his deep blue eyes had faded.

"Well, I'd better be going. I've got physics next hour."

"Yeh. Well, see ya." Adrienne nodded.

With a backward wave, Kyle sauntered off down the hall. Her eyes didn't leave the wide, athletic expanse of his shoulders until he turned into the physics lab.

The Brain was kind of cute!

The foreign thought was cut short by Jill who came racing up to Adrienne's side.

"Did you get him? Did you find the snake?"

"Yep! Under the bleachers. He's back in his home."

"Oh, Adrienne, you're so brave!"

"Brave? Don't be ridiculous, Jill. It's just a snake."

"Ugggh!" Jill shuddered. "A cold, slimey, slithery snake."

"They aren't slimey. You should feel Melvin. He's smooth and cool."

"No thanks. Anyway, we have to figure out our biology display so we can tell Mr. Palley what it's going to be. And," Jill gave Adrienne a glare, "it will have nothing to do with snakes."

Adrienne only smiled and steered her friend toward an empty science lab.

At four-thirty, Adrienne bounded from the school bus and hurried across the yard to her mother.

"Hi, Mom. Whatcha doing?"

"Loading up these curtains for the cabin. I thought I'd put my old set of cookware out there, too. No use having our guests rough it *too* much. Go change and we'll take the jeep."

"No need to change. My clothes look pretty grubby already." Adrienne rubbed ruefully at her sweatshirt.

"My goodness, child! What did you get into today?" Naomi's eyes grew large as she took in her daughter's dirty clothing.

Adrienne opened her mouth to speak, then decided against it. It would be difficult to explain. Her mother was not fond of snakes.

"Long story, Mom. Let's just get going to the cabin."

Naomi, too preoccupied to be curious, nodded briskly and climbed into the open jeep. Adrienne scrambled after her.

The road to the cabin was rough and twisted, gnarled like an aged tree limb from harsh Minnesota winters and disuse. Adrienne felt her teeth rattling in her head as they bounced and jounced toward the far reaches of Fuller property.

"Goodness only knows why anyone would want to come out here, sit in an unheated cabin and hunt," Naomi muttered. "Recreation, they call it. I call it crazy."

Adrienne bit her lip and smiled. Just as long as

her college fund kept growing, these hunters could stay forever.

As the jeep navigated the path that circled in front of the house, the cabin seemed oddly unoccupied. Silent. Dark.

Adrienne shivered. The vacant windows of the cabin stared at her like curious eyes. The fine hairs at the back of her neck prickled and stretched like fur on a startled cat's back. She felt as though someone—or something—were watching.

Oblivious to her daughter's rigid pose and strained expression, Naomi swung out of the jeep and began hauling boxes toward the cabin.

A flutter of movement inside the house caught Adrienne's eye. As she watched, a small mop of plain brown hair began to rise over the sill of the window. It was followed by a pair of inquisitive brown eyes. Then appeared a pair of round, apple red cheeks and the curious, pursed mouth of a toddler.

Adrienne shook herself. Of course! The child of the hunter! She'd let that first odd impression of silence and foreboding alarm her. Disgusted with the overactive imagination that played such tricks on her, she flung herself from the jeep and ambled toward the cabin.

"That must be one of our new guests." She tipped her head toward the window. It was empty.

Almost before that fact could register, the door of the cabin swung open revealing the small boy. But he was suddenly jerked away from the portal with a force that made Adrienne gasp.

Inside the cabin she could hear scolding. "I told you not to open the door, Jeffrey! You must never open the door!"

Suddenly the owner of the voice filled the doorway. His expression held a tinge of anger and of something else. Nervousness? Fear?

"What can I do for you?"

Naomi had missed the entire exchange while she bent over the filled boxes. She straightened, extended a friendly hand and replied, "Welcome to our cabin. I'm Naomi Fuller. I've brought your curtains and some kettles."

The large man visibly relaxed. His shoulders slumped and the tense expression on his face melted. He took Naomi's hand. "Thank you. Thank you very much."

Adrienne studied his profile. He was the jumbo version of his small son—from the mop of brown hair to the expressive brown eyes. But he appeared pale, not red-cheeked and robust like the boy.

"My daughter and I will hang the curtains and then get out of your way. I know how you men like to be up here alone communing with nature, but a few curtains will keep out that morning sun."

Naomi bustled right past, not noticing the frown that marred the man's features. Adrienne followed at a much more cautious pace. He didn't seem terribly happy to see them. Surely it wasn't because of the curtains.

Adrienne felt a tugging at the hem of her sweater. She glanced down to find a wad of her sweatshirt clutched in the fist of the little boy.

"Hi, there."

"Hi."

"What's your name?"

The child hesitated. Then he glanced at his father in a slightly bewildered manner before responding, "Name's Jeffrey."

"Jeffrey? That's a nice name."

The child nodded. "What's yours?"

"Adrienne."

"Oh."

The conversation ground to a halt. Adrienne

turned to help her mother with the windows. Jeffrey and his father watched.

"You have another boy, don't you Mr.—"

"Wilson. Ed Wilson. Ted is out hunting up firewood."

"My husband will bring some up this evening. Then we'll leave you alone to do your hunting."

"Much obliged."

Adrienne wondered exactly what it was he was obliged for—the firewood or the promised privacy.

Naomi persisted. "My husband says you're a former teacher."

"That's right."

"And that you plan to tutor your boys while you're up here."

"That's right, too."

"Don't you think they'll miss a lot, being away from school this time of year?"

Adrienne wanted her mother to stop talking. Mr. Wilson looked irritated, almost angry. But his voice was level when he answered.

"Boy's going to learn more about nature up here than in a dozen science classes. I'm a former science and math teacher myself. He'll be weeks ahead of his classmates."

"Well, I'm sure you know best," Naomi commented absently as she patted the last of the curtains into place. "There, now. Doesn't that look much better?"

All four of them were standing back, admiring her handiwork when a tall boy burst through the cabin door.

"Pa, I got the wood and I . . ."

He was about her age, Adrienne could tell. Tall, slender, and brown-haired like his dad. He looked more like his dad than his little brother, Adrienne decided. It was funny how both boys looked like their father yet they didn't really resemble each other.

His eyes weren't as brown as Jeffrey's. His face was more angular and expressive. It was a pleasant looking face, a kind face.

"These are the Fullers, Ted. They've hung the curtains."

"Oh."

These men had a way of stopping a perfectly good conversation mid-stream, Adrienne decided, wishing it weren't so. Ted Wilson looked like a nice boy to get to know. Interesting, too. There was an expression in his eyes that made her curious. It was the same look Jeffrey had had when she'd asked him his name: Bewildered, a little frightened, unsure.

Yes, indeed, Adrienne would certainly like to get to know Ted Wilson better.

Chapter Two

"I will not touch that—that *thing* . . . for all the A-plusses in the world!"

"Come on, Jill! It's no big deal. You'll get used to it. You have gloves on."

"I wouldn't touch it if I were wearing armor. Get that thing away from me!"

"Don't talk that way about my friend PorkChop. He's part of my ticket to med school. If we do this display for the biology department professionally enough, maybe somebody will notice me and mention it to whoever gives out scholarships. There's always a chance."

Adrienne's expression was hopeful as she dangled PorkChop closer to Jill's nose. Formaldehyde fumes wafted around both girls like curls of fetid smoke.

Jill blanched and closed her eyes. When she opened them, the well-preserved fetal pig was still in sight.

"I just can't touch him, Adrienne. He's so—"

"Piggy?"

"Very funny. You're going to have to dissect him alone."

"Then you can do the frog, the rat and the earthworm."

"Brrrcccctgggghhhh!"

"What'd you say? I think you just invented a new sound."

"I can't dissect anything. I won't. No one can make me."

"Except Mr. Palley."

"I'll quit school."

"And the truant officer."

"I'll run away from home."

"Will you write?"

"Very funny. Verrry funny."

"Mr. Palley was delighted when I told him we'd do a display comparing the internal systems of an earthworm, a frog, a rat and a fetal pig. All we have to do is open them up and find the little parts that perform the same function in each body. It'll be a breeze. We'll make nice colorful backboards, read up on anatomy and be ready to give a lecture. It will look great on my résumé for college."

"I'm going to be an interior decorator. I have no need for skills in dissecting fetal pigs on my résumé." Jill crossed her arms over her chest. "And I won't do it."

"Hello, girls," Mr. Palley greeted the two. "Getting ready to start your display?" He beamed like a newly lit lighthouse. He turned to Jill. "I'm very pleased to see you taking an interest in this project, Miss Wainright." His voice lowered in warning. "It should help you pull out of the grade slump you've been suffering in this class."

Jill swallowed.

Adrienne grinned and tucked her chin into her lab coat.

"Working together I expect you girls to have a fine display. It should be an excellent addition to Science Day here at the school. If you need any help, just let me know." He wandered off, his hands nestled deeply into the pockets of his lab coat.

"PorkChop and I are going to give you one more chance," Adrienne crowed to her friend.

"I can't stand it," Jill whined as she pulled on her lab coat. "I just can't stand it."

"How's the surgery coming?"

A ripple of instinctive pleasure played down Adrienne's spine at the sound of the low male voice.

"Fine. But I lost my assistant."

"Jill Wainright, you mean? Are you sure you aren't better off without her?"

Adrienne wanted to defend her friend against Kyle's remark, but she knew, deep down, that he was right. "It's going to be okay. She'll get used to it."

"Yeh, but when? Before the display is finished?"

"I hope so." Adrienne lifted PorkChop's dissecting tray and slid it into a large plastic bag. "She's more squeamish than even I imagined."

"So how come you don't just do the project on your own? Let her do something else? Collect leaves or something?"

"She's got to get extra credit on this display in order to make up for a test she failed. I can't let her flunk."

Kyle shrugged. "I suppose, but just don't let it hold you back. I think you could go far in science."

Adrienne studied him from beneath hooded lids. Go far? Was that "The Brain" speaking?

"Thanks. What makes you think so?"

"You have good facility with scientific terms. You're perspicacious, insightful and quite discerning. I think you have potential." Kyle ticked her attributes off on his fingers.

"Translated into understandable terms, does that mean you think I'm smart?" The irritation in her voice was softened by the smile on her lips.

Kyle had the grace to look chagrined. "Yup. Smart."

"Thanks, I think. When you start to talk like that, I just want to switch you off like a bad song on the radio."

"Habit. I've listened to my dad for too many years."

"You mean there's someone else who talks like that?"

"My whole family, actually. Dad's a chemistry professor at the junior college and my mother is a psychotherapist. It's like changing cultures every time I go home."

"Sounds terrible to me." Adrienne's own family was as down-to-earth, God-fearing and normal as one could get.

Kyle grinned. "Not so bad, really. You get used to it. When I was a little kid I thought every little boy was told to be quiet with the words, 'Modulate your expressions, dear.' "

Adrienne giggled. He was nice when he could laugh at himself instead of being so all-fired serious. And cute too. He had a dimple in his left cheek when he smiled. His blue eyes were dancing. She shifted her weight to lean back on the slate-topped lab table.

"I suppose you're entering the senior division of the fall science fair."

"Planning on it."

"Whatcha going to do?"

"Something with pollutants and the bird population. The title isn't completely worked out yet."

"I thought you'd have it all figured out by now . . ." Adrienne hesitated before adding, "being The Brain and all."

"Is that what I am? 'The Brain?' " His eyebrows arched until they disappeared under his dark blond thatch of hair.

She shrugged. "Guess so. It's a compliment, isn't it?"

"Maybe. Or maybe it's like you said the other day."

"What was that?" Adrienne couldn't remember anything she'd said being important enough for The Brain to remember.

"You said I was too smart for everyone else."

"I didn't mean it like it was bad or anything."

"It is if it keeps you from making friends."

Adrienne shot him a curious stare. "Does that happen to you?"

"What do you think?"

She swallowed. She knew *she'd* let his reputation come between them. She'd pigeonholed him in some compartment for people who were too intellectual to understand. Did everyone do that?

"Sorry."

"Don't be. I'm also smart enough to confront people who can comprehend my situation."

Just then Jill came upon them as they grinned at each other in a comradely, conspiratorial fashion. Jill's head swiveled from one to the other in amazement.

"I came to put PorkChop away," she announced lamely. "I thought I'd practice touching him."

"Great! Put him in the cooler, second shelf. I've already put our names on the pan," Adrienne instructed.

Jill nodded and gingerly picked up the pan and its unwanted burden. Kyle and Adrienne watched her back into the walk-in refrigerator with a grimace of distaste blanketing her features.

Impulsively, Adrienne volunteered, "We're going to start the backboards for the display tonight. Mom said she was going to bake today. There should be something good in the house to eat. If you want to come over and give us artistic advice you're . . ." as the full impact of what she was saying hit her she paused, shyly, "welcome."

She wanted to crawl under the table and shrivel into a ball. Why had she gone and done that? Just because he was nicer than she'd expected him to be, more vulnerable, she'd gone and made a fool of herself. Why would a smart, good-looking senior boy—especially The Brain—want to come and watch two sophomore girls make posters for a science display?

He was entering the senior division of the fall science fair. She wasn't even eligible to do that yet. Her own project would have to wait until the spring contest. He had a chance to win and make a name for himself. Suddenly the class display with PorkChop and the hope for good comments on her transcript seemed young and silly.

Adrienne jutted her chin forward a bit and looked up. Let him say no. It was stupid of her to have asked.

"I'd like that very much."

"It's okay, I didn't expect—what?"

"I said I'd like that very much."

"You would?" She couldn't keep the disbelief from her voice.

"I would."

"Ah, okay then," she stammered. "Any time after seven. My folks have Bible study tonight. They said I could have company while they were gone."

"I'll be there." Kyle smiled and scraped a lock of wheat blond hair away from his forehead.

Adrienne felt a red hot blush of pleasure licking its way across her cheeks.

Just as Jill returned, Kyle leaned close to Adrienne and murmured, "See you tonight." Jill's eyes grew round as frisbees, but she refrained from speaking until Kyle sauntered out of earshot.

"What was *that* all about?"

"No big deal. Kyle's coming over tonight, that's

all." Adrienne tried to ignore the tickle of pleasure in her rib cage.

"That's all? The Brain is coming to visit? I thought we were going to make posters tonight!"

"We are. He's just going to come and keep us company."

"Great," Jill muttered. "PorkChop and The Brain, all in one day. What next?"

Adrienne turned her head away from her friend and smiled. She'd wondered that too.

By five minutes to seven Adrienne's insides had revolted. Warring troops had taken sides in her midsection and nervous muscles were contracting around her supper. She was afraid she was going to be sick.

"Why are you so nervous, anyway?" Jill asked through a mouthful of chocolate chip cookie. "You see The Brain in school every day and all of a sudden he's making you uptight."

"All of a sudden I've found out I kind of like him," Adrienne admitted. The statement surprised her as much as it did her friend.

"Like as in, 'he's not so bad' or as in, 'I *like* him?' "

Adrienne swallowed. "I don't know. Maybe the second. He's just nicer than I expected."

"Well, you two should be perfect for each other. Too smart for your own good. Future doctors. Future famous inventors. But," Jill stuffed the last of the cookie into her mouth, "I think all those brains are *boring*."

Adrienne gave her friend a cross glance. "It's those brains that are going to save you from flunking biology, you know. His and mine. He'll probably be able to tell us all sorts of things to improve the display."

Immediately repentant, Jill straightened. "Okay. So forget I said that. Maybe we can find something to do with The Brain around that's not boring."

"His name is Kyle."

"Sorry." An impish grin flickered across Jill's features. She stretched backward in her chair and tilted it until only the back legs were resting on the floor. "Adrienne Fuller. This is the first time in our whole lives that I've ever seen you interested in a boy!"

Adrienne grinned back. "Not so. I'm interested in two others."

Jill's eyes grew round and her mouth puckered. "Who?"

"The Wilson boys."

"Who are they?" Jill's freckled nose wrinkled in bewilderment.

Adrienne chuckled. "They and their father are living in the cabin this fall."

"Oh, them." Jill waved her hand airily. "Now you're trying to change the subject."

"I did a good job, too," Adrienne announced, turning to the clutter at her feet. "Now, then, do you want to do the stenciling or the artwork?"

Jill sighed and settled herself onto the floor. "Stencils, of course. I don't even like the thought of *drawing* PorkChop's interior."

The girls were so engrossed in their work that both jumped when the doorbell rang.

"Kyle!"

"The Brain!"

Adrienne gave Jill a warning look as she scooted for the front door.

"Hello."

"Hello, yourself."

Kyle stood at the screen door, his hands balled into fists and buried deep in his pockets. His blond hair mopped over his wide blue eyes. Adrienne hadn't noticed his still deep summer tan until now, as bronze skin peeked from beneath his pale blue shirt. Her heart did an excited little flip-flop as she opened the door. How had she ever managed to consider him uninteresting?

"Come on in. We're just getting started."

"Are you sure I won't be interrupting?"

"Positive. And anyway, Mom made chocolate chip cookies and sweet rolls today. You can eat while we work."

Kyle grinned. Adrienne liked it when he smiled.

The smile grew as he viewed Jill stretched across the living room floor surrounded by discarded tagboard and felt tipped pens. There was more color on her hands and face than on any of the paper.

"I think these pens are leaking," were Jill's words of greeting.

Adrienne bit her lower lip. If Jill didn't need the help so badly, she would have loved to work on this alone. Adrienne was methodical, Jill was haphazard. Adrienne was meticulous, Jill was sloppy. Adrienne was intrigued by the project, Jill was bored. But she was also Jill's best friend and only hope of passing biology. She wouldn't give up now. And next year she'd be old enough to qualify for the senior competition at the fall fair and have a project of her own.

As her mind raced ahead with the dream, her eyes fell on the voiceless TV screen flickering in the corner. "Hey! There's Mr. Rand, the game warden, on television!" She hurried to turn up the volume.

The interview was just beginning.

". . . Game warden Bertrand Rand of Hartwell County is with us this evening to discuss the illegal poaching situation at the north end of the county."

"Hey! That's us!" Jill piped. All three pair of eyes were riveted to the screen.

"There have been numerous reports of poaching recently, sir. Would you comment on this situation?"

Mr. Rand looked nervous with the microphone held toward his lips like a big metal lollipop. He cleared his throat and began.

"Hunting season usually does bring out a few dishonest folks. Normally it's the fellow who doesn't tag his deer until he sees a game warden coming or shoots something other than the bird in season and tries to sneak it home and into the oven. But what's been going on lately is quite a bit different."

"Could you expand on that, sir?"

"Carcasses of various animals and birds have been found and reported. Deer, elk, moose, out-of-season birds. We think they were abandoned because someone was approaching and the poachers were forced to leave their kill. I'd hate to think how many animals they must have gotten away with."

"Duck hunting season is upon us now. What influence will that have on your search for the poachers?"

"As you know, poaching is the killing of any animal or bird outside of its designated hunting season. It's going to get worse now that everybody and their brother is out with a gun. But we'll get these guys. We'll get 'em. . . ."

Before Adrienne could move to turn off the television, Rand's image faded to gray and was replaced by the picture of a young child. The announcer's voice intoned, "Tonight on our public service feature 'Have You Seen This Child?' is Ricky Riverias. When he was last seen, Ricky was two years old, had dark hair and brown eyes. He was—" Adrienne leaned forward and flicked the switch.

"Hey! Why'd you turn that off?" Jill yelped.

Adrienne's hand moved slowly from the television's controls. "I don't like all those missing children ads. You can't get away from them. They're on everything from milk cartons to the ten o'clock news. It's depressing."

"But not worse than having your child or brother

or sister missing," Jill pointed out.

"No. But it bothers me to think about it."

"Are you two going to talk all night or get at least one poster finished?" Kyle interjected.

Adrienne gave him a grateful glance. Those ads made her very nervous somehow. It frightened her that someone would be so cruel or desperate that they would steal a child. It turned her insides to ice. Anyway, Jill had already forgotten about either Sheriff Rand's story or the missing child. Her head was bent low over PorkChop's vital statistics.

By nine o'clock, with Kyle's advice, the posters were actually showing promise. Jill packed up the leaky markers in a shoebox and stacked the backboards near the door.

"Gotta go. I hear my brother's car coming. Thank your mom for the cookies."

"Okay, see you tomorrow on the bus." Adrienne opened the door for her friend. She found Kyle next to her as the taillights of the Wainright's receding car disappeared down the Fuller lane.

"Suppose I'd better be going, too."

"You don't have to. I think there are still some sweet rolls left in the kitchen."

Kyle grinned. "You talked me into it. Anyway, I wanted to ask you a question."

He didn't say any more until they were settled at the kitchen table. Adrienne looked at him expectantly, swirling her spoon in a cup of hot chocolate.

Kyle cleared his throat. Once. Twice. And again.

Adrienne crossed and uncrossed her legs at the ankles.

Finally, he spoke.

"Remember, you asked me earlier today if I were going to enter the science fair?"

She nodded.

"I've got the title worked out now."

The news hardly surprised her. Adrienne wondered why it made him so nervous to talk about it.

"What *is* your project?"

Kyle's eyes lit up. "I'm thinking of calling it 'The Effects of Chemical Pollutants and Mercury in Air and Water on the Bird Population of Hartwell County.' I'm basically going to study the loon, the cormorant and the kingfisher because they are primarily fish eating birds."

"Wow!" Adrienne's eyes grew wide with admiration.

"I've actually been working on this for nearly a year. I banded some birds last fall and did a lot of work this spring during the nesting season. I just wanted to take my observations full circle to the point where I started last fall."

"What have you learned so far?" Adrienne breathed, fascinated. This was exactly the kind of thing she would have loved to do. Her respect for Kyle mushroomed.

"There are some birds in this area that may really be threatened by the chemicals in the air and water. The chemicals accumulate in the birds' bodies from eating poisoned fish or insects. My cousin works with the Minnesota Department of Natural Resources. They're the ones who do the state water quality stuff. He's been sending me their reports and told me how to check our local water for pollutants and pesticides.

"Those chemicals can cause any number of reproductive problems for the birds including poor fertilization or the laying of eggs that are too thin-shelled. If the eggs break before hatching, the numbers are bound to drop. I did a count last fall and another this past spring. The third count should tell me if my suspicions are true."

"You should be watching the birds at the north end of our property," Adrienne enthused. "There must be more there than anywhere else in Minnesota."

"I'd like to. You'll have to take me up there."

Adrienne glanced across the table. Could she believe what she was hearing?

Then Kyle dropped the bombshell. "In fact, I *was* going to ask you if I could do some observing on your property." His eyes shifted to her face, "And also if you wanted to help me."

"Me?" Her voice came out in an embarrassing squeak. "You want *me* to help *you*?" The Brain was asking for her help?

He nodded. "I've been thinking about it ever since we went looking for Melvin. You've got a good head on your shoulders, you're patient and you seem to like living things. I want to do another bird count and I'd like some help. Will you?"

Would she? She gazed at him blankly. What an opportunity! She could observe Kyle right along with the birds and learn exactly how to do a similar project next year. It might be one more step toward medical school.

"I'd give you credit with Mr. Palley for helping me," Kyle offered. "I know you and Jill promised to do that display for the biology room. But, since sophomores can't enter the competition, I thought you might be interested. I wouldn't expect you to work on my project without telling him. Maybe you could get some bonus points or something. . . ." His voice trailed away.

It occurred to Adrienne that her silence had made him afraid she was going to say no. With a shock, she realized he had no idea how honored she felt that he'd asked her.

"I'd love it! When do we start?"

Kyle laughed. "Saturday all right? That will give you some time to study the bird book so you know what you're looking at. And time to ask your dad if it's all right to go stomping across your property."

Adrienne shrugged. "The hunters from the cabin go wherever they please. I don't see why we can't. We're not going to hurt anything."

Kyle's expression grew serious. "You're lucky to have that cabin rented—especially with the poaching trouble they've been having in the area. It makes it harder for anyone to be sneaking around your property shooting illegally when there's a house at that end of the land."

"I suppose so. We've never really thought about it like that. It's Dad's way of adding to my college fund; and until this year, the same people have rented it. They're just like old friends."

"Who's in it now?"

"Some people named Wilson. A father and his two sons. They answered an ad in the Minneapolis paper. There's a boy my age and a little guy, about three."

"Doesn't the older boy have to go to school?"

"Guess not. His father's a teacher. He's tutoring him at the cabin while they stay there. His dad said he'd learn more about nature in a month here than in a year at school."

"Maybe he's right," Kyle shrugged, "but it seems like it would be lonely to spend a month like that."

The questions that always floated to the surface when Adrienne considered the threesome at the cabin reappeared. But it was not her worry. She'd hardly seen either boy. What their father had decided would be best for them must be all right.

Pushing the thought from her mind, Adrienne walked Kyle to his car.

The night was warm and clear. The hint of wind wrapped itself around Adrienne's shoulders like the lightest brush of cashmere. The night sounds made a chorus around them.

Adrienne inhaled deeply of the wonderfully fresh

and verdant aroma. The fragrant, earthly smell of fall was in the air. A frog chirrupped and creaked from a nearby slough. An owl hooted from the lush thickness of the trees behind the house.

Then the tranquil moment vanished.

Kyle's head came up and his eyes met hers as a sharp "bang" broke the peaceful moment.

For a moment, Adrienne did not want to imagine what it was. The crack of a rotted tree falling. The backfiring of a car. The slamming of a door. But as her eyes met Kyle's she knew her first instincts were correct.

The sound was gunfire.

Chapter Three

Kyle's lips tightened into a grim line. Adrienne turned to him with a question in her eyes.

"Night poachers?"

"Maybe."

"Or maybe one of the neighbors saw a skunk in the yard."

"Could be." Kyle sounded doubtful.

"But you don't think so?"

"You heard what the game warden said about the poaching."

Adrienne nodded.

Night poaching, or "shining," was a cowardly way to hunt game if anything was. The hunters would shine the headlights of their cars or a flashlight into the eyes of the creature they were stalking. When it was blinded by the sudden bright light, it was easy to bring down with a single shot. There was no sense of adventure or fairness or morality about shining. None at all.

"Maybe I should stay until your parents get home," Kyle offered. "Will it bother you to be alone?"

Adrienne had insisted she was fine, but as his car disappeared down the lane, the large empty feeling in her midsection threatened to engulf her. It was with relief that, moments later, she saw her parents' car pull into the driveway.

"Mom! Dad! Hi!"

"A welcoming committee at our front door? What's going on?" Her father threw his jacket across his shoulder.

"Did you know there was some poaching going on?" Adrienne blurted.

Wayne's gaze danced over his daughter's face. "Yes, Adrienne. I did."

"We heard gunshots tonight, just as my friend was leaving."

Her father smacked his palms against the tops of his thighs. "It's happening that close, then. Tomorrow I'd better go out and look around. Could you tell from which direction the shots were coming?"

"Not really. Kyle might know." Then she added hopefully, "Could the sound have been something else?"

"Doubtful, considering the amount of trouble we've been having in this area. Somebody is making big money on the animals they're pulling out of here. The game warden is doing the best he can, but it's a large area to cover with lots of places to hide. Those guys could go on leeching our wildlife for a long time before they're caught."

"Daddy—" Adrienne began, but he cut her off.

"You'd better get yourself to bed, Adrienne. There's nothing to be done tonight. I'll call the sheriff and tell him you heard shots. That's all we can do."

Somberly, she nodded. She climbed to the second floor of the old farmhouse. Without turning on her light, she entered the room that had been hers since birth.

The window was open and the sheer curtain ruffled and swayed in the night breeze. Adrienne moved softly across the big rag rug that covered the floor and perched on the window sill.

The night sounds accosted her ears once again. A hooting owl. A chirping cricket. The wail of a distant timber wolf. The sounds had been tarnished somehow. The melody of nature had been fouled by a sour note. A note of violence.

Adrienne stared into the thick blackness, relieved only by the stars and the glow of the moon. What was going on out there, anyway? What kind of wicked men were hatching illegal plans? She shivered. The night was no longer a safe black cocoon. It was a dark curtain hiding evil.

When she opened her eyes, it was to the light of morning. She could smell bacon frying.

"Good morning, sleepyhead. I thought you were going to laze about all day." Naomi Fuller's head came around the door jamb.

"What time is it?"

"Nearly seven-thirty. You're going to have to hurry in order to get ready for the bus."

Adrienne bolted out of bed as though the mattress had suddenly turned to a bed of nails. "Why didn't you get me up sooner?"

"You were so restless last night that once you finally settled down I hated to disturb you."

Adrienne paused in her hasty dressing. "I kept dreaming about the gunshots and the poachers."

"We don't even know that what you did hear was a gun, Adrienne. It could have been a car backfiring on some little country road."

"Maybe," Adrienne agreed hesitantly.

"Well, it could have been. Just don't go worrying yourself about it. Your father will deal with it. Come on downstairs and eat."

Adrienne pulled on a lemon yellow tee shirt and a long white cardigan. Then she dug in her jewelry box for a pair of lemon and white earrings. Once they were in place, she gave herself a long look in the mirror.

Not bad, she thought, if only she'd had time to tame her spikey bangs and the wild ruff of a mane her mother called hair. A grin split her features. Everyone was used to her eccentric clothes and hair. Why fuss today?

Kyle Rogers—that was why. She wanted to show him just how nice she could look. But there was not time to do anything about her hair, so she tied a yellow ribbon through the most unruly parts and shrugged. Let people think she'd *planned* her hairdo this way. And, with a bit of her characteristic independence, she thought, let Kyle think whatever he wants.

"You look like lemon meringue pie today," was her father's greeting. He was dressed in jeans and hiking boots, a bright plaid lumberjack shirt and hunting cap.

"And you look like Paul Bunyan."

He chuckled. "Wish I had legs as long as our fabeled lumberjack. I'm going to do some walking around the property today to see if I can find any evidence of unwelcome visitors."

"Maybe the new people at the cabin have seen something."

"I'll check with them, too. But don't go worrying your head about this, Adrienne. Nobody's going to dare come near the house or the well-used trails."

She finished her breakfast in silence. It wasn't the thought of anyone coming to the house that frightened her. Poachers were a cowardly sort—doing their dirty deeds in secret, sneaking away from the scenes of their crimes. They didn't scare her.

It was the animals and the birds. Adrienne could barely tolerate to see a beautiful doe or buck, dead and sightless, strapped to the roof of a car or thrown into the back of a pickup. She wanted to cry when a hunter displayed a string of bloodied birds like a trophy.

She understood the necessity for keeping the animal population down so that hunger and disease didn't ravage the herds and flocks. She understood the ecological reasons that made hunting acceptable. But she couldn't bear the thought of the hurt and injured animals that inexperienced hunters maimed each year. And she couldn't look at the beautiful and graceful creatures dead.

God's creatures. It just didn't seem right.

She was particularly quiet on the bus. Jill was bouncing in her seat like a ball of silly putty, rambling about everything from the Science Fair to the dress her mother had brought for her from Minneapolis. Kyle's seat was empty.

Finally, when they were only blocks from the school, Jill noticed her friend's silence.

"What's with you today, Adrienne? You've hardly said a word!"

"Tired, I guess. I didn't sleep very well last night."

Jill looked at her curiously. "Too many thoughts about," and she lowered her voice, "The Brain?"

Adrienne gave her friend a withering look. "You know better."

Jill flashed a broad, metal-decorated smile. "I wouldn't blame you. Actually, he's kind of nice—when he doesn't use those big words."

Adrienne's eyebrow arched.

"And cute."

Adrienne's other eyebrow joined the first.

"Is this Jill Wainright putting her stamp of approval on Kyle Rogers?"

"For you. Not for me. I'd like to meet someone who doesn't talk like a dictionary." She was silent for a moment before adding, "How old did you say that boy staying at the cabin was?"

"Jill!"

"All right, all right. Just wondering."

Adrienne looked at her friend fondly. Jill was one of those "people" persons. That's why Adrienne liked her. It was also why she was struggling so in biology. Jill refused to concentrate on anything that didn't have the promise of fun connected with it.

Adrienne smiled to herself. For her, biology *was* fun. Everything about it. Even working with Jill on a science display. . . .

"Jill! Our display!" Adrienne bolted upright in the seat.

"Yeh, what about it? We've got plenty of time."

"Well, we do, sort of."

"What do you mean 'sort of'?"

"I'd planned to try and get our project together and Kyle asked me to help him with his too. We'll have to get ourselves organized so that. . . ."

"The Brain asked you for help?" Jill didn't even attempt to keep the amazement from her voice.

"Is that so hard to believe?" Adrienne inquired with as much dignity as she could muster.

"That's not what I meant," Jill stammered. "You know that."

"Then what did you mean?"

"The Brain is so . . . brainy. He uses all those big words. The teachers love him. Why would he need help with school work?"

"Maybe he doesn't. Maybe he just needs a friend."

"Oh." Jill turned thoughtful. "Maybe he does."

Adrienne was very pleased to be the person he'd chosen.

She was even more pleased after Mr. Palley responded to the news that she and Kyle would be working together.

"Wonderful, Adrienne! I think you can learn a lot from Kyle." Mr. Palley had beamed on her like a lighthouse beacon onto dark waters. "And I have great hopes for your future."

The future. Adrienne turned the phrase over and over in her mind.

The future was so important to her because it involved so many people. It involved the faceless, nameless people that were crying out for help all over the world. As a doctor, she could do something to stop the suffering she watched on the evening news and read about in the news magazines that came in the mail.

As you did it to one of the least of these my brethren, you did it to me.

That command from Matthew had captured her imagination and her spirit. Now every step she made inched her closer to her dream of becoming a doctor. And Kyle was becoming a part of her journey.

"Ready to go birdwatching?" Kyle had a pair of impressive-looking binoculars strung around his neck and a funny red and white hat with a navy blue brim on his head. He wore cutoff jeans and a fish net tee shirt. He looked more like a lifeguard than a birdwatcher.

"Aren't you afraid of scaring off the birds with your hat?" Adrienne inquired primly. She'd spent nearly an hour getting ready for their first big outing. She was a little put out that Kyle dressed like he was attending a party in a rag-bag.

She'd chosen her softest, most broken-in stonewashed jeans and a matching denim shirt with rhinestone studs in the collar and cuffs. Adrienne had even succumbed to wearing tiny rhinestone buttons in her ears and polishing her nails a soft, sheer pink.

"Nah. We're going to get snagged and dirty." He paused to study her. "You look too pretty to be going out in the woods. Are you sure you don't need to change?"

Adrienne grinned. "Thanks but no thanks. I don't have a hat to compete with yours."

He raised a finger to the rim. "Very perspicacious of you."

"Huh?"

Kyle grinned. "Discerning, insightful, astute."

"What?"

He threw up his hands in mock dismay. "Very *clever* of you, Adrienne!"

"Then why didn't you *say* so?"

"I did."

"In normal words, I mean."

A thoughtful look came over Kyle's face. "I'll try from now on, Adrienne. I know I intimidate people with my vocabulary. Will you remind me if I slip?"

"Gladly," Adrienne laughed.

"Good. Now we'd better get going. I'm hoping to spot a lot of birds before the afternoon is out."

The forest already hinted at fall. There was a faint, musty smell in the woods, a clue that autumn was quickly nearing.

Breathlessly, Adrienne called to Kyle, "Can't we sit down for a minute? My legs are about to give out."

Immediately, his pace slowed. "How about sitting right here?"

"Anywhere. Anywhere at all."

The two of them rested against a fallen scrub oak and Adrienne crossed one leg over her knee to knead her ankle.

"Did you twist it?"

"A little. I was trying to keep up with you when you spotted that owl."

"Just tell me when I'm moving too fast."

The two of them sat together in comfortable silence. A chorus of forest noises surrounded them.

Finally, Adrienne spoke. "How did you get so interested in the forest, Kyle? You seem to know the name of every tree and every blade of grass."

He smiled slightly, a wistful, thoughtful smile. "I spent most of my childhood in the woods. It was my escape."

"Escape from what?" Adrienne couldn't remember anything she'd ever wanted to escape from as a child—except doing dinner dishes, perhaps.

His sky-blue eyes grew somber. "Home."

"Home?" That was an answer difficult for Adrienne to understand.

Kyle turned to study her. The lines of his face were tense. "My father always expected a great deal of me, even when I was small. Sometimes I needed to get away."

"But your mother . . ."

"My mother worked a lot. Dad came home early. He was in charge of the house—and me—most of the time."

"And he was strict?"

"Very." The way Kyle said it left no doubt.

"I'm sorry."

Kyle moved nervously on the log. "He didn't hurt me or anything. Dad would never do that. He just wanted me to be a little grown-up. And he wanted me to be perfect." Kyle chuckled ruefully. "I sure haven't done a good job with that one."

"So you came out here to get away from having to be perfect?"

"Something like that." He smiled. "At least this was *one* of the places I liked to come."

"Where was the other?" Adrienne was curious. This was a new Kyle that she was meeting, a sensitive, vulnerable boy she'd never dreamed existed.

"I'd go and see Bob Martinson."

"Pastor Bob?" Adrienne gasped. "*My* Pastor Bob? But I've never seen you at church!"

"I don't go to church. My parents don't approve.

They don't like it that I hang around the parsonage, but they haven't stopped me from doing it yet."

"But why?" Adrienne breathed. It was something she could hardly imagine.

Kyle shrugged. "My parents are both scientists. They think everything should have a scientific explanation. Faith in Christ resists explanation."

"What about you? What do you think?" The question hung on the damp air of the forest.

He turned and smiled at her. "I'm counting on faith."

Adrienne expelled a little gusty breath of relief. She put her hand atop his as it lay on his thigh. "I'm glad."

A new understanding grew between them as they sat there in the verdant lushness of the forest. Now there was another common bond to cement their friendship, something more lasting and more precious then either could explain.

Adrienne unconsciously shook her head. Life was full of surprises. And she had a hunch that the boy next to her was full of surprises as well. There was still a lot to learn about Kyle Rogers.

She was dirty and sore from head to toe when Kyle dropped her off on her front step late that afternoon. Adrienne was still trying to brush away the dirt and leaves that clung to her jeans when her father stepped onto the porch to greet her.

"Hi, Kiddo. Find a lot of birds?"

"Millions of them." She'd never realized the bird population of northern Minnesota could be so large. And Kyle was able to identify every single winged creature he spotted. "I spent most of the day with my nose in the bird book. I don't think I was any help to Kyle at all."

Her father chuckled. "Sometimes being pleasant company is help enough."

"Do you think I'm that? Pleasant company, I mean?"

Her father lowered himself heavily to the porch step. Adrienne noticed the tense lines that bracketed his mouth and the cloudy, distant expression in his eyes.

Her father turned to her, "I'm sorry, Adrienne, I'm afraid I wasn't listening. What did you say?"

Immediately Adrienne knew something was amiss. Her father always listened. *Always.*

"What's wrong, Dad?"

He turned to her with a grim expression. "That transparent, huh? You can tell something's wrong?"

"You can't fool me, Dad."

"Never could, Adrienne. You were smart as a whip from the day you were born."

"And you could never put me off the track, either. Don't try and distract me. What's wrong?"

Wayne Fuller stretched his long legs down the porch steps until the heels of his work boots rested in the powdery dust at the foot of the stairs. The little metal pliers he kept hooked in a loop on the leg of his overalls tapped against the wooden step. A late-living dragonfly looped and shimmered near her ankle. The yard was quiet.

Her father answered her question with another question.

"Did you and Kyle see anything unusual in the woods today?"

"Unusual? What do you mean?"

Wayne shifted uncomfortably. "Just what I said. Anything seem to be out of place? Different?"

Adrienne's brow furrowed in thought. "I don't know what you mean, Dad. Everything looked pretty much the same to me."

Her father nodded thoughtfully and sank back

into the somber pose he'd held since he sat down beside her.

Finally Adrienne bristled. "What's going on here, anyway?"

Wayne Fuller turned to his daughter. He studied her carefully. Adrienne always knew when her father was contemplating something, for it was his habit to run the tip of his tongue around the edge of his top teeth. He was doing it right now.

After a long silence he spoke.

"I found a carcass of a dead buck today."

Adrienne's stomach did a flip-flop.

"In fact," Wayne continued, "I found signs that there had been several animals butchered. The buck was the only whole animal left. Otherwise it was mostly entrails and . . ." he paused at the sick look on Adrienne's face. "Anyway, I just wanted to know if you and Kyle had seen anything like that in the woods."

"No, nothing."

"Good. But maybe you kids had better stay out of the woods for a while."

"Poachers?"

Wayne nodded. "They're getting pretty bold. They were hunting not too far from our farmstead."

"But there are people living in the cabin, Dad. It should be safe to go up there to look for birds."

Her father gave a disgusted snort that made Adrienne jump.

"Is it? I wonder. I'm afraid our new renters aren't a good deal of help."

"But why?" Adrienne couldn't remember ever before seeing her father so upset.

"I was up at the cabin today after I found those signs that the poachers were stepping up their activity. I thought Ed Wilson should know so that he could be on the lookout for them, too."

"What did he say?"

"Not much." Wayne shook his head. "That Wilson is a strange duck if I've ever seen one. Didn't seem interested at all that someone was illegally killing off the wildlife in the region."

"He didn't care?"

Wayne shrugged. "Maybe he did. I'm not sure. He seemed more interested in whether or not this poaching problem would cause any publicity in the region. He wanted to make sure no policemen or newspaper reporters started to invade his privacy. I don't really think he cared about the animals at all. He was more worried about being left alone."

Adrienne frowned. She wasn't accustomed to such a selfish attitude. How could someone *not* care about the animals and their destruction? What could be more important than that? Unless . . . The active wheels of Adrienne's imagination began to turn. Unless the new renters had something of their own to hide. Perhaps something that had to do with the poaching itself. . . .

"Dad?"

"Yes, honey?"

"Do you wish the Sandshills had come back to the cabin again this fall?"

Wayne Fuller turned worried eyes on his daughter.

"I certainly do." His voice seemed to echo through the quiet farmyard. "I certainly do."

Chapter Four

All night a kaleidoscope of disturbing images whirled through Adrienne's dreams. The patter of rain on her window beat out a staccato rhythm. The cabin. The odd and mysterious Wilsons. The body of the dead deer. Her father's worried frown.

She woke from her troubled sleep more curious than ever about the suspicious events on the farm. Curiosity had one and only one effect on Adrienne. It gnawed at her until she found some way to answer the questions that plagued her.

As her feet swung to the soft green carpet of her bedroom floor, she resolved to do some investigating of her own.

"What would you like for breakfast, dear?" Naomi Fuller was already pouring orange juice when Adrienne padded into the kitchen.

Adrienne wore a cable-knit cotton sweater of moss green and dark brown jeans. She'd chosen her clothing to blend with the bleak and rainy face of the forest on that dreary morning.

"Toast is fine. And an egg. Or pancakes. If you have any sausage, that is." Adrienne felt especially hungry today. Anticipation, no doubt, fueled her appetite.

Naomi hid a smile. She knew by Adrienne's appetite when she was up to something. But then again, Adrienne was usually up to something.

Adrienne bolted down the stack of pancakes her mother set before her, barely conscious of the food she was chewing. Her eyes were glued to a rivulet of moisture meandering down the kitchen window.

"Did it rain a lot last night?"

"Twenty hundredths of an inch. Just enough to make everything soggy."

"Can Jill and I go for a walk in the forest today?"

"Won't you be cold?"

"I'm dressed for it." Adrienne plucked at the stitching of her sweater. "I'll tell her to bring a jacket."

"I suppose. Just don't go too far—and stay on the trails." Her mother left the rest of the warning unsaid.

Adrienne bobbed her head thinking, *Just as far as the cabin, that's all.*

She sprung from her chair to call Jill.

When Jill answered the telephone, Adrienne whispered, "Are you ready to help solve a mystery?"

There was a long pause at the other end of the line.

"Adrienne? Adrienne Fuller? Are you playing a trick on me?"

"No, I'm serious!"

"What mystery?"

"I can't explain right now. You'll have to come over."

"Now?"

"Of course, now! And wear something warm."

Adrienne sensed Jill's suspicion even over the phone, but after a few moments of silence, Jill's curiosity overcame her. "Oh, all right, but this had better be good."

Adrienne was already on the front steps when Jill arrived.

"So, what's this big mystery you're talking about?"

Jill threw herself down next to Adrienne on the porch swing.

"Dad found a carcass in the woods. The poachers are increasing their activity in this area."

Jill's eyes grew wide. "I don't want anything to do with any poachers, Adrienne. They might be dangerous!"

"We aren't going to 'catch' anybody, silly. We're just going to see if we can gather some clues."

"What kind of clues?" Jill's eyes slanted suspiciously. "What have you got going on in your head, Adrienne Fuller?"

Adrienne sighed. She'd have to explain.

"Dad didn't like the way Mr. Wilson, the man who's renting our cabin, was behaving. He didn't seem to care about the poachers at all, just whether or not the word was going to leak out and wreck his privacy."

"So?"

"Doesn't that strike you as odd?"

"Maybe he doesn't like wildlife."

Adrienne gave her friend a get-with-it stare.

Jill's eyes grew round. "You think maybe *Wilson* is a poacher?"

Adrienne shrugged. "Who knows? Anyway, I'm supposed to be helping with the cabin. I thought I'd take an extension cord to the Wilsons. They might want to use the electric heater to get the dampness out of the cabin."

"That's as good an excuse as any," Jill commented. "Then I can meet that Wilson boy—Ted."

Adrienne nodded, but her thoughts were not on Ted Wilson. Her thoughts were on what they might find.

The day seemed meant for mystery. The forest was eerie and dank. The rain-clouded sky loomed above them and the thick green leaves were heavy with moisture. Adrienne shuddered, not from the cold and wetness seeping stealthily into her clothing, but from something less tangible and more alarming. Anticipation? Fear?

"I don't like this, Adrienne. This place gives me the creeps," Jill whined pathetically.

"You've been here a hundred times before."

"Not when it's been raining, I haven't. It's spooky when it rains."

"You think everything is spooky. Rain. Porkchop. Worms."

"Eccckkkk!"

"Now what's wrong?"

"Worms! Look at how they're coming up out of the ground!" Jill stubbed her toe at a pink and wriggly creature curled on the ground.

"They do that in the rain, Jill. They like moisture."

Jill buried her chin in the collar of her coat. "I hate worms. Why do I let you get me into these things, Adrienne?"

Adrienne grinned over her shoulder at her soggy, forlorn friend. Poor Jill. Then Adrienne put a finger to her lips.

"Shhhhh. We're getting close to the cabin."

Her statement was accentuated by a clap of thunder.

"It's going to rain again!" Jill's wail blended with a gust of damp air.

Adrienne shivered inside her sweater. It *was* pretty miserable out here today. Even she had to admit that. But that was the best kind of day for exploring, when no one would dream that sleuths would be out.

A jag of lightning split the sky overhead and another, closer, clap of thunder made both girls gasp. Adrienne could see Jill's face pale another shade lighter.

"Come on, the cabin isn't very far. We can go in there until the storm is past." Adrienne patted the extension cord inside her sweater. It had been her excuse to come to the cabin. Now it was her ticket to warmth. The clouds opened and doused them with a torrent.

There was a dim light in the window of the cabin, a frail beacon to the two chilled girls. As they neared, a face peeked over the sill and two round dark eyes widened in surprise at the sight of the bedraggled pair.

Little Jeffrey. Adrienne was so glad to see signs of life and warmth that she gave a soggy little laugh of relief. The laugh turned to a moan as she saw Jeffrey's older brother roughly jerk him from the window and pull the shade closed. A knot of apprehension started to build in Adrienne's stomach. Wasn't he even going to let them inside?

Adrienne pounded on the cabin door with a closed fist.

"Go away." Ted's voice could just be heard above the rain.

"It's raining!"

"Go away." His voice was flat, emotionless, unwelcoming.

"We're soaked to the skin. Can't you help us?" Jill pleaded. Her teeth were beginning to chatter from the icy dousing.

"I said, go away. Now."

Through her anger at the rude and thoughtless treatment, an odd and out-of-place thought came to Adrienne. Ted sounded frightened! Of them? How could he be? What threat could two soggy fifteen-year-old girls be to him?

A gust of wind waggled the leaves of the big tree over the doorway of the cabin. The accumulated rain-water on the wide leaves spilled onto the two of them like a cold shower. Adrienne's curiosity gave way to anger.

She pounded madly on the door. "Ted Wilson, you let us in to dry off! This is my father's cabin and you're just renters. You can't treat us this way. We're freezing!"

Jill, who had been very quiet during this little episode, began to cry.

"Come on, Jill," Adrienne pleaded. "Don't cry. We can always walk home and get dry clothes."

"My shoes are all squishy," Jill wailed.

Adrienne tried not to listen to her friend's muffled sobs as she pounded on the still-closed door. Then, between raps and Ted's desperate commands that they leave, another sound intruded.

Footsteps.

Heavy, alarming footsteps. Adrienne and Jill shrank against the side of the cabin. Adrienne glanced wildly about, searching for a place to hide.

A man appeared through an arch of trees to the south of the cabin. He was wearing old army fatigues, thick gold and green rubber boots and a soggy felt hat, the brim of which had sagged with dampness and hung limply around his face. Adrienne couldn't see his eyes.

The scream which had been building in her throat died out. Her body felt constricted with terror.

"Hello, girls. What are you doing out here?"

Adrienne felt a surge of relief flood through her body. Her knees went rubbery with relief. Ed Wilson! The boys' father! All her suspicions about him were allayed for a moment by the friendliness of his voice and the prospect of dry shelter.

"We got caught in the rain and he wouldn't let us in," Jill stammered, tilting her head toward the cabin. Her teeth were chattering like a pair of trick false teeth while raindrops and tears mingled on her eyelashes.

"Well, it's a good thing I came along when I did, then," Wilson commented jovially. He dug deep into the pocket of his trousers and brought out a key. Unlocking the door, he ushered the girls inside.

Ted and Jeffrey were standing at the far corner of the room. Jeffrey was wide-eyed and curious. Ted had his hands placed protectively on his little brother's shoulders, his own eyes wide with another emotion. Fear.

"Ted, you should have let these girls inside. It's pouring out there," Wilson chastized.

"But you said—" Ted began.

"Never mind. When young ladies come to call, you're supposed to act like a gentleman." Adrienne glanced at the man in disbelief. Even *she* didn't believe a word he was saying.

"But you—" the boy began again.

"Get these girls some towels and dry clothes. After they change they can tell us why they were out in this part of the woods on such a nasty day." Now Wilson's voice carried an edge of warning.

Adrienne was suddenly thankful for the extension cord tucked into the waistband of her jeans. As she shook the moisture from her sweater, the cord tumbled to the floor.

"We came to give you this extension cord. We thought the cabin might be extra chilly in the rain and you'd like to move the portable heater into the middle of the room. We didn't plan on getting all wet and cold ourselves."

Ted and his father exchanged a glance. Adrienne could see them both evaluating her reason for appearing at the cabin. Imperceptibly, Mr. Wilson's shoulders relaxed, then Ted's. Instinctively she knew her reason had been accepted.

"That was very nice of you."

"It's okay. I'm supposed to help with the cabin. The

rental money goes into my college fund."

Wilson smiled, a genuine smile now. "Good. It's nice to know our money will be going to a worthy cause."

For a brief moment he seemed genuinely pleased for her and almost fatherly. She liked him for that.

Then he pasted that saccharin-sweet smile on his face and the thought vanished. He was being *too* nice, she observed. He couldn't be *that* glad for an extension cord! They were hiding something. More than ever, Adrienne wanted to find out what it was.

"Here's some of my clothes you can put on." Ted handed each of the girls a pair of jeans and a sweatshirt.

"But these are almost brand new!" Jill gasped. "We shouldn't borrow these. Don't you have something older and more worn?"

As Jill fussed over the nearly new clothing Ted had handed her, Adrienne watched the expressions on the two elder Wilson's faces. Ted looked uncomfortable and unsure. A worried frown passed over his father's features.

Finally Ted spoke. "It's okay. I don't mind. My other stuff is dirty right now. Take this."

Jill reached for the clothing. She was obviously eager to get into something warm and dry. Only Adrienne seemed to have noticed the odd tension when Jill pointed out the newness of Ted's clothing. It was another stray fact for Adrienne to tuck into the back of her mind. Perhaps someday she could figure out the Wilsons.

"Would you girls like a cup of hot chocolate?"

Adrienne and Jill had changed into Ted's too large but oh-so-warm clothing. Some of the chill was finally abating.

"You bet!" Jill had recovered from her fright.

"That would be great," Adrienne agreed. Their excuses for hanging around the cabin were dwindling. Soon they would have to leave. Adrienne was still looking for clues—to what, she wasn't quite sure.

"Feeling better?" Wilson asked as he set steaming mugs on the table in front of the two girls.

"Much!" they chimed together.

Then, to Adrienne's surprise, Jeffrey Wilson tugged timidly on the arm of her sweatshirt.

"Yes, Jeffrey?"

"Can I sit on your lap?" the little boy inquired. His eyes were large and sad looking.

"I'd like that." Adrienne pushed her chair away from the table and Jeffrey scrambled into her lap. Contentedly, he rested his head on her shoulder.

"Well," Mr. Wilson cleared his throat. "Looks like Jeffrey's found a friend." The thought seemed to make him uneasy.

An idea flashed into Adrienne's mind.

"Could I come and see Jeffrey again sometime? Maybe we could play games or—"

"Well, I don't know," Wilson hesitated.

"I could bring some play-dough and we could make dinosaurs."

"Please, Daddy?" Jeffrey clapped his hands together in delight.

Emotion played across Wilson's face. "Maybe some afternoon, son."

"Soon?"

"We'll invite Adrienne for the afternoon very soon."

Jeffrey clapped his hands, delighted with the answer. Adrienne was not so delighted. *Invite.* They would *invite* her to come to the cabin. Didn't they want her wandering in unannounced?

Jeffrey put the palms of his hands to Adrienne's cheeks. "I invite you to come and see me anytime. Okay?"

With one sweet sentence he'd undone all this father's tricky plans, Adrienne mused.

"Thanks, Jeffrey. Now we'd better get home so my parents don't worry about us." She set the little boy on the floor. "And thanks for the dry clothes."

As the two girls walked from the cabin, Adrienne could sense three pairs of eyes boring holes into their backs. She breathed a sigh of relief when they were out of sight.

"Well, what did you think?" she asked Jill.

"They were nice. I don't think there's any big mystery there."

"Then why wouldn't Ted let us into the cabin?"

"I dunno. Because his dad told him not to, I guess. My folks don't want me letting strangers into the house when they aren't home."

Jill's answers did nothing to settle Adrienne's ever-present curiosity. A mystery surrounded the Wilsons and she wanted to discover what it was.

Halfway home Adrienne felt a raindrop on her nose.

"Oh, oh. If we don't hurry we're going to be wet all over again."

"Too late," Jill murmured, lifting her eyes to the canopy of clouds.

The skys opened and another drenching downpour dumped its fury on the two girls' heads. The rain was hard and pelting, like needles pricking the unprotected skin of the girls' faces. They began to run.

The forest was noisy with a persistent thrumming as hard pellets of rain pummeled the leaves. For a moment, the two paused under a tree to catch their breath.

"If I get out of this without a case of pneumonia, Adrienne Fuller . . ." Jill warned.

"Shhhh. Just pull the sweatshirt over your head and—what was that?" It was a noise foreign to the forest. The crack of a gun.

The two girls stared at each other.

"Is that what I think it was?" Jill whispered.

"We've got to get out of here," Adrienne hissed.

"Which way?"

"I don't know. Toward the farm, I guess. We're almost halfway there already."

The two tiptoed through the carpet of leaves and fallen branches that littered the forest floor. This part of the woods was as familiar to Adrienne as her own back yard. Actually, it *was* her back yard. But today an alien, unknown element hung about it she had never sensed before. Something had changed.

Jill forged ahead through the trees until Adrienne lost sight of all but quick flashes of her red-sweat-shirted back.

"Eeeeeekkkk!"

Earthworms again, Adrienne thought to herself. *When is Jill ever going to grow up?*

But it was not earthworms that had frozen Jill into a posture of terror. She stood rigid and still in a tiny clearing in the trees. Adrienne approached her huffily, about to give another lecture about the harmlessness of the oligochaetous worm, but her step slowed to a halt as she saw what lay at Jill's feet.

Another deer. A young stag, the nubbins of his horns still in velvet. Dead from a bullet. Adrienne could see the blackened hole in its neck through which the bullet had entered.

"Run, Jill! We've got to get out of here—*now!*"

The two girls careened headlong through the forest. The trees whizzed past them with dizzying speed. Occasionally, one or the other of them would fall, tripped by an outcropping root or a fallen branch. Adrienne could hear Jill's sobs as they ran. Or were they her own?

Scratched and frightened, they burst from the woods into the cleared area of the Fuller farmstead

still clutching their bundles of soggy clothing. . . .
Safety at last.

Adrienne turned and stared back into the silent
woods from which they had just come, filled with a
sense of fear and foreboding. Something was wrong
in her beloved forest. *Terribly wrong.*

Chapter Five

"Hey! What's with you two?"

Kyle was standing near his father's station wagon in the Fuller's driveway.

"Kyle! The poachers! They've killed another buck. We came across it in the woods."

His gaze traveled from one distraught girl's features to the other. "Did you see anything else?"

"No. We heard gunfire and decided we'd better get home fast. Jill stumbled on to the deer in a clearing."

Adrienne glanced at her friend, then took a harder look. "Jill, are you okay?"

"I want to get dried off. These clothes are as wet as the first set."

"First set?" Now Kyle was really curious.

"We were in the woods when it started to rain—" Jill began.

"And the boy at the cabin didn't want to let us in—"

"But his father made him—"

"And they gave us some clothes—"

Before they could continue, Kyle held up a hand. "Why don't we go inside where it's dry to hear the rest of this story?"

Adrienne led the way. The house was silent. A note

on the kitchen table informed her that her parents had gone to town for groceries.

"Where are parents when you really need them?" she groused. "We have to tell Dad about the buck. It should be reported to the game warden. Maybe he could still catch whoever—"

"They're long gone by now. I heard you two screaming your lungs out long before you popped out of the trees. You've scared away all the poachers in three counties."

"Maybe the poachers aren't as far away as you think," Adrienne commented, watching Kyle's face carefully as she spoke.

"And what does that mean?"

"Maybe they're still on the land."

"And what makes you think that?" He sounded doubtful.

"Oh, don't pay any attention to Adrienne," Jill interrupted. "She thinks those Wilsons at the cabin have something to do with the poaching, I know she does."

He turned to Adrienne. "Do you?"

"Something's very funny out there, Kyle. Ted Wilson was just plain *scared* to let us into the cabin. I think he's afraid of his dad."

"His dad was perfectly nice to us," Jill insisted. "He smiled a lot and everything."

"He smiled *too much*. But he never looked very happy. He wanted us out of the cabin, Jill. I'm sure of it."

"Well, I don't know anything about that, but I do know that I'd like to meet this Ted Wilson."

Both girls turned to Kyle in surprise. "You would?"

"Sure. I'd like to know what his dad is teaching him while they're out here in the woods. He might even be able to give me some information for my science research. I think it would be most beneficial to spend a month in the woods and acquaint oneself with the flora and fauna and—"

"Come on, Jill. He's not taking me seriously and he's talking *like that* again. Let's get changed."

Kyle grinned. "And while you do, I'll call the game warden to tell him about the deer."

Adrienne nodded glumly. Couldn't anyone else even *sense* that something weird was going on?

She didn't feel any better in her dry clothes. She still had that pervading sense of trouble that had haunted her all day.

She fingered the sleeve of Ted Wilson's damp sweatshirt before tossing it into the dryer. She would have to go back to the cabin. She'd missed something, some clue, as to why the Wilsons were so secretive. And the sweatshirt and Kyle's curiosity about Ted were her tickets into the Wilson home.

The girls padded barefoot into the kitchen. Adrienne was toweling some of the moisture from her hair.

"What did the game warden have to say?"

"I left a message with his answering service. Apparently this poaching thing has got him really busy."

"Kyle," Adrienne began, not quite sure how to approach her request.

"Yeh?"

"Ted's clothes are almost dry. I don't suppose he packed too many changes for the cabin."

"So?"

"Do you want to go with Jill and me to return them?"

"I'm not going back into those horrible, spooky woods! Not with the poachers around!" Jill announced.

"Kyle's probably right about our making so much noise that they won't be within ten miles of here by now," Adrienne coaxed. "And we have to return the clothes sometime."

"I don't like it," Jill protested. "Not one bit."

"And Kyle could come with us. We'd be perfectly safe with him along."

Kyle chuckled and squirmed on the edge of the seat he had taken at the kitchen table. "Now I'm a knight-in-shining-armor! What next?"

"You know what I mean," Adrienne chided. "I think we should go back to the cabin soon."

Kyle thoughtfully chewed at the corner of his bottom lip. "I have to go home tonight. I just came by to drop off another bird book. But I suppose I could go with you girls tomorrow afternoon."

"Perfect!" Adrienne crowed.

"I'm never going back," Jill complained.

"Don't then. Kyle and I can go alone." Adrienne glanced from the corner of her eye at her friend. If that approach didn't work, nothing would. Jill disliked being left out more than anything else.

"I suppose if the rain stopped and the sun came out it wouldn't be so bad. . . ." Jill admitted.

Adrienne grinned inwardly. Aloud she said, "Let's meet here at three o'clock. That will give us enough time to change from our church clothes and have dinner. Then we can go to the cabin and deliver the clothes." To herself, she added, *And find out what's really going on with Ted Wilson and his father!*

Ted and his strange father were far from Adrienne's mind the next morning as she got ready for church. The sun was shining, the sky was clear blue and cloudless, the day fresh and crisp.

Eagerly, Adrienne shrugged into her church clothes and ran a brush through her thick mane of hair.

"Toast is ready, Adrienne," her mother called from

the bottom of the stairs. It was a Sunday morning tradition at the Fuller house—wheat toast with home-made preserves, orange juice and coffee for her parents. Then, after church, they would all go to Othello's Cafe for brunch.

Adrienne smiled. Othello was really a very small and unprepossessing man by the name of Herbert Granger, but when he moved to town, he named his new restaurant Othello's. "A touch of class, that's what this town needs," he always announced when questioned about the grandiose name. His wonderful Sunday brunches had certainly supplied that.

Sunday was Adrienne's favorite day. Food for the soul and then some for the body, her father maintained. Her feet flew down the steps to the kitchen.

"My, don't you look nice today?" Naomi commented proudly.

"Thanks, Mom. But don't you think these sleeves are a little short?" Adrienne pulled at the cuffs of her pink oxford cloth shirt. "Or am I just used to wearing big, baggy clothes and this is how it's supposed to fit?"

"You're growing again, my dear." Mrs. Fuller eyed the classic oxford shirt and trim burgundy jumper Adrienne wore. If it weren't for the burgundy, pink and black striped stockings her daughter sported, she would have looked almost traditional. But Adrienne was never quite traditional.

"No doubt about it," her mother continued. "I thought you'd be done with that by now. I suppose this means another shopping trip."

Mother and daughter turned their heads toward the sudden sputtering coming from the pantry adjoining the kitchen.

"Wayne, are you all right?" Naomi asked, the concern heavy in her voice.

"Did I hear you link the words 'Adrienne' and

'shopping trip' in the same sentence?" Adrienne's father had a plaintive look on his face as he entered the room. "An entire swallow of coffee went down the wrong pipe just thinking about it."

Adrienne grinned. "Cheer up, Dad. Once I get into medical school, there won't be any money left over for shopping trips. Maybe I'll have to wear the same things for a few years!"

"Thanks, I think." Wayne grinned.

Adrienne knew how much her parents wanted her to become a doctor—almost as much as she wanted it for herself. She was sure already that her family was a team—and they'd all work together to see that she fulfilled her dream. Silently she gave a word of thanks for their supporting, caring affection.

Her feet were tap-dancing a restless beat against the floor of the Fuller automobile by the time they reached the church. Adrienne's eyes scanned the parking lot. She gave a gasp of surprise to see Kyle's car parked near the church.

Already seated, he was obviously and painfully alone. Adrienne felt a tiny surge of pity when she saw Kyle's deep blond head several pews ahead. The least his parents could have done was come with him. Then she grinned to herself. He must be a sleepyhead on Sunday mornings, the curls at the nape of his neck were still damp, as though he'd just gotten out of the shower in time to leave for church.

As she settled herself between her parents, her eyes stayed on Kyle's wide shoulders; but once the service started, her attention was drawn to the front of the church.

Adrienne loved the music and the words of the service. Together they wove a wonderful, hopeful picture in her mind and heart. She lost herself in the service. In what seemed like only moments, they were being ushered from the sanctuary.

Adrienne edged nearer to Kyle in the foyer of the church. She wondered where his parents were. And she wondered what they thought of their son's insistence at attending church.

Adrienne's speculation was sidetracked when Kyle, looking very serious and well-behaved, winked at her. It was all she could do to keep from winking back.

"I'm meeting my parents at Othello's for lunch," he mouthed.

"We're going there, too!" she mouthed back.

"Meet you."

"Okay." Adrienne's heart was doing flip-flops in her chest. Finally, she was going to meet Kyle's parents.

Othello's was full to the point of bursting when the Fullers arrived. Fortunately, Naomi had reserved a table near the back, and the family trooped through the crowd to be seated.

"This is a bigger table than I reserved, Wayne." Naomi brushed a stray hair from her forehead.

"I suppose we should offer to share it. It's awfully busy in here."

Timidly, Adrienne interjected, "Kyle's family is waiting for a table. That's only three more. Could they sit with us?"

"Why don't you go ask them?"

Adrienne shot out of her seat and hurried to the spot where the Rogers family waited.

"Hello, I'm Adrienne Fuller," she began. "Kyle and I go to school together. We have a big table we'd like to share. Would you like to have brunch with us?" It was a big speech to give, considering how Mr. Rogers was staring at her.

Martin Rogers seemed to be turning the invitation about in his mind. Finally, a small vestige of a smile quirked his lips.

"Thank you. Your cordial hospitality is very much appreciated. We would be delighted to join you. Shall we convene at your table?"

Adrienne struggled to keep her eyes from flying wide open. So that was where Kyle had learned to speak like a dictionary! She squelched a giggle.

As they wound their way through the clutter of tables, chairs and people, Adrienne could hear Kyle's father giving him a lecture.

". . . please watch your manners, young man. These people have been kind enough to extend an invitation to our family. It is your duty to represent us in a seemly and becoming manner."

"Kyle has beautiful manners, Martin," Mrs. Rogers interjected meekly over her shoulder. It was the first time Adrienne had heard the woman's voice.

"Only because of our watchful upbringing, dear. If not closely supervised, children can become unmanageable."

Adrienne caught Kyle's eye. He looked miserable.

Thankfully, she and Kyle found seats at one end of the table while her parents separated them from Mr. and Mrs. Rogers. After they'd traveled to the buffet and said grace, she and Kyle were able to talk.

"Is he always that strict?" she whispered, not wanting anyone else to hear.

"Sometimes worse."

Her heart went out to her friend. Kyle didn't have it much better than those two frightened boys in the woods.

The woods! Adrienne snapped her fingers together.

"Kyle, can you still go to the cabin?"

He glanced cautiously at his father who was engaged in a lecture directed at Adrienne's parents. "I think so. My homework is done, plus a lot of extra credit things. I don't have to do errands on Sunday. It should be fine."

"Good! There's something really funny going on at that cabin, Kyle. I can just sense it. There's something odd between Ted Wilson and his father."

Kyle looked at her for a long moment. When he spoke, his words were oddly accentuated. "Not everyone has a relationship with their parents like you do, Adrienne."

Adrienne felt like sinking into the floor and disappearing from sight. If she'd run into Kyle and *his* father in the cabin instead of the Wilsons, she'd probably be suspicious of them, too. Mr. Rogers was so stern and intimidating.

But, she told herself, there was a difference. Kyle was respectful and wary around his father, it was easy to see that. But Ted Wilson was something else. Ted Wilson was *afraid.*

"I can't believe I'm doing this. I've got to be losing my mind. I don't know how you ever talked me into—"

"Put a cork in it, Wainright," Adrienne said cheerfully. "You know very well you're dying to go to the cabin. You think Ted Wilson is cute and, anyway, you're as curious as we are to find out what's going on up there."

"But it's like a *swamp* in the woods today! I'm going to wreck my new shoes and it's going to be all your fault. I can't believe . . ."

Kyle and Adrienne exchanged a knowing glance over Jill's head as she bent to examine her white high-topped Reeboks. Jill had been grumbling and complaining ever since they'd met, but she'd also been walking briskly, eagerly, toward the cabin.

Adrienne fingered the articles of clothing she'd placed in her red duffle bag. They were her ticket into the cabin and to the answer to all her puzzling questions.

The forest was still sodden from the rain. A damp, musty smell permeated the air. Absently, Adrienne's eyes rested on a familiar gnarled scrub oak. Her step slowed.

"Kyle!" she hissed.

"What is it?"

"I think this is where we found the carcass of the deer. I remember that tree because it reminded me of a little old man."

His step slowed and he glanced around. "Any sign of it?"

"Nothing. Not anymore." Adrienne felt an odd, sick feeling in the pit of her stomach. She and Jill had been very close to the poachers. Too close. Perhaps they had even listened in on the conversation between her and her friend. Adrienne felt a creepy, crawly feeling shimmy up the back of her neck. What horrible thing was happening in her beloved forest?

She was silent as the trio made its way deeper into the woods. The familiar childhood haunt seemed strange and new, filled with danger and intrigue. Adrienne experienced an unpleasant thrill of fear.

"Well, do you think he'll let us in?" Jill's voice broke through Adrienne's reverie.

They were nearing the cabin. It was as dark and vacant looking as ever, the window shuttered against intruders. If she hadn't known better, Adrienne would have guessed that it was empty.

Only a pair of discarded galoshes by the door hinted that there was someone inside.

"There's only one way to find out," Adrienne responded. She pushed herself forward and raised her fist to rap on the door.

From the corner of her eye, Adrienne could see the window shade move. Ted's eyes, wide and startled, peered from beneath one corner of the curtain. Adrienne stared back.

After what seemed like a long time, the door opened.

He spoke through the crack in a rough, unwelcoming voice.

"Whatdayawant?"

"Hi, Ted. How are you today?" Adrienne tried to make her voice as pleasant and unthreatening as possible.

"I said, 'What do you want?' "

"We came to visit. It was such a nice afternoon, we didn't want to stay home."

"I don't want visitors."

". . . and we brought back the clothes you loaned us when we got wet. Don't you want them?"

The door opened a hair farther.

"Hand 'em over."

"Nope. Don't you know it's not nice to be so rude? Aren't you going to invite us inside?"

Adrienne could see the confusion and the hesitation in Ted's eyes. He wanted to let them in, she knew. He was obviously lonely. But something was keeping him from throwing the door wide open.

"My dad said . . ."

So Mr. Wilson was absent again. Where did he go when he left his sons alone?

"I know, you aren't supposed to let strangers into the cabin. But we aren't strangers. My dad owns this cabin. It's how we're earning money for my college education and medical school. Surely he wouldn't mind *us*!"

Adrienne felt a little guilty using her most persuasive powers on Ted, but nothing less would work, she was sure.

"Well, I guess not." The crack widened another notch. Adrienne could see Ted's little brother hanging on to Ted's pant leg. She stuck her toe in the door so that he could not close it again.

"Maybe we could even play a game or something. I didn't bring any play-dough for Jeffrey, but there are lots of games in the cedar chest at the foot of the bed. Monopoly. Scrabble. I got new games from my cousins for Christmas and so we put the old games out here for the renters. Do you like games, Ted?"

"Game! Games!" Little Jeffrey began to clap his hands and dance about the room. Ted looked at his brother, then longingly through the door. Finally he seemed to make his decision. He swung the door open.

"Come on in, then. But if my dad finds you here when he comes back from fishing and bawls me out, you can't ever come back. Promise?"

"Promise." Adrienne gave him her hand somberly. She didn't want to make trouble for the boy. She wanted to circumvent it. Could she make him believe the three of them really did want to be his friends?

The cabin was neat and clean. It was as though Ted and Jeffrey had spent their day scouring every corner and straightening every dish. Adrienne grew somber. Perhaps they *had*.

Then she clapped her hands together and inquired with the enthusiasm of a cheerleader. "Which first, Monopoly or Scrabble?"

"Mop-oly! Mop-oly!" Jeffrey cheered. Ted dove to get the board.

After a heated discussion over who was going to be the top hat and who was going to be stuck with the artillery cannon, the foursome and little Jeffrey sat down to play. Once the decision had been made to let the visitors into the room, both Ted and Jeffrey seemed delighted to have a diversion.

Adrienne even forgot to wonder what it was that Mr. Wilson had told his sons to strike such fear of strangers into them.

"Not Boardwalk again!" Ted wailed. "I'm going to have to mortgage everything I have. Why'd you put so many houses on Boardwalk, Jill? I'm going broke."

Jill clapped her hands with glee. "Make you a deal, let's merge, become partners and see if we can bankrupt these two—"

"Whoa!" Kyle chuckled. "No corporate raiders in this game! Anyway, it's getting dark and we'd better get home."

Adrienne glanced out the window. The hours had spun by. She turned to Ted, who was laughing over some private joke with Jill. It had been a very nice afternoon. Normal. Adrienne suspected Ted hadn't had many normal afternoons. At least not lately.

"We gotta go. My dad will be furious if I'm late," Kyle announced. That made Adrienne's feet move doubly fast. If Mr. Rogers was always as stern as he'd been today, she didn't want Kyle in any trouble with him because of her.

"Bye," Ted waved from the doorway. "And . . ." his voice faltered, then grew stronger, "thanks for coming."

The threesome exchanged glances as they disappeared into the cover of the forest. They hadn't uncovered any big mysteries at the cabin—just two very normal, and very lonely, boys.

They ran helter-skelter through the forest, racing against the oncoming darkness. All three were panting when they collapsed on the Fuller porch.

Jill chattered on about the afternoon and how nice Ted was, seeming to forget Kyle's presence entirely. Adrienne wanted to stuff a fist into her friend's mouth. Kyle Rogers wouldn't want to hear all of this girl talk.

But Kyle didn't seem to be listening. Even Jill finally stopped chattering to ask, "What's wrong, Kyle?"

He pulled himself out of his thoughtful silence to answer, "I think we just did something very foolish."

"Foolish? Going to see Ted? Why?"

"Not going to see Ted. Coming home so close to dark."

"But I don't understand. . . ." Jill's voice trailed away. Suddenly she *did* understand. And with terrifying clarity, so did Adrienne.

"You mean you think we were in danger?" Adrienne whispered, hating the idea even as she spoke it.

"It just occurred to me that the poachers could be anywhere. It's probably a good thing that we were racing and yelling and making a lot of noise. If we'd been more quiet and startled them . . ."

Adrienne's blood felt cold and shivery in her veins.

"You think that they might have . . ." She couldn't finish the sentence.

"Hurt us? Or worse? I don't know Adrienne. I don't know how desperate these men are." Kyle was somber.

Desperate. The word hung on the evening air. Unbidden, a question came to Adrienne's mind. Were Ted Wilson and his father desperate too?

Chapter Six

"You don't *really* think the poachers might have been close to us . . . do you?" Jill sounded very young and unsure.

Kyle shrugged. "It was inexcusable of me not to think more clearly. We should never have stayed at the cabin this long. My cognitive powers—"

"Talk to us, Kyle—on *our* level," Adrienne reminded him gently. Most of the time he was doing better, talking like a teenager instead of a textbook.

Kyle smiled. "All right. I goofed. I wasn't thinking. Coming through the woods at dusk could have been really stupid. I imagine that's the time the poachers come out—just before sundown, when the animals begin to graze."

"Well, *I* think we were in danger all afternoon," Jill announced importantly, watching her friends receive the pronouncement.

"And just what do you mean by that?" Adrienne wondered. Had Jill's fluffy little head gone completely to seed?

"I think that we were in one of the poacher's cabins all afternoon." She crossed her arms and dared either of her friends to deny it.

"Ted and Jeffrey?" Kyle mocked. "Come on, Jill, be real."

"Not Ted and Jeffrey! Mr. Wilson. He sneaks around in the woods all day. He's never there with his boys and they aren't supposed to open the door or speak to anyone. What is he afraid of?" Jill paused for proper effect. "Getting caught, that's what!"

Kyle and Adrienne exchanged glances. She could see by his eyes that he'd already considered that possibility. And she knew the thought had crossed her own mind more than once. If flighty, illogical Jill had come to the same conclusion, it must be a fairly obvious conclusion. Still, they couldn't have Jill spreading that idea all over town.

"I wouldn't say that to too many people if I were you," Adrienne warned.

"I agree with Adrienne, Jill," Kyle added softly. "That's a very harmful statement if it's not true."

Jill's lower lip came out in a pout. "Well, why else would he want to be so secretive and mysterious?"

Adrienne and Kyle barraged Jill with possible solutions.

"Lots of reasons," Adrienne offered. "Maybe he doesn't like crowds."

"Or people in general."

"Maybe he's had a nervous breakdown and needs the rest."

"Or one of the boys has been sick and needs to be quiet."

"He could like to wander in the woods and watch the wildlife like Kyle."

"Do I look like a poacher?" Kyle inquired.

"Quit ganging up on me. You know very well you don't trust him. I promise not to say anything to anyone if you think I shouldn't, but . . ." and Jill's voice faded.

"But what, Wainright?"

". . . but I think that we should investigate a little more ourselves."

For a moment, Adrienne couldn't believe what her normally timid friend was saying, then the proverbial light bulb flashed on in her brain.

"You want to spend more time with Ted Wilson! That's it! You don't care about any investigating! You just want an excuse to go and visit him!"

"Do not," Jill protested, but her voice was weak. Adrienne knew immediately that she'd read her friend correctly.

"That's okay," Adrienne assured her. " 'Cause no matter what your reason is, I think we *should* do a little sleuthing. After all, it's my dad's cabin and my college money involved here. And," Adrienne paused, "the animals."

"Aren't you girls biting off a little more than you can chew?" Kyle interrupted. "Shouldn't you leave this to the sheriff or the game warden?"

"We won't get in their way. And maybe we can help." Adrienne turned to face Kyle. "And we'll feel lots safer if *you* help us."

Kyle rolled his eyes. Adrienne tried to hide a smile. He was so cute when he was, and she used one of Kyle's own big words, exasperated.

"Oh, all right. I have to do the birdwatching anyway. And I don't want you two barreling off on your own and getting hurt."

"Your science project is the perfect reason to be wandering around in the woods. Nobody's parents can complain about birdwatching!"

"Let's make a pact, then!" Jill crowed, delighted to have an excuse to know Ted Wilson better. "To the investigation!"

She stuck her right hand out before her. Slowly, Adrienne placed her own hand on top of her friend's. Groaning, Kyle rested the palm of his hand against the top of Adrienne's and Jill lead them in a solemn shake.

As their fingers parted, Adrienne tucked her hand into her pocket and turned away. Her stomach was doing little flip-flops of pleasure. A pink blush stained her cheeks. She hadn't counted on liking the feel of Kyle's hand on hers quite so much.

The investigation seemed doomed from the start.

One thing after another delayed the day when the threesome could spend a day in the woods birdwatching—and people watching.

Jill bolted through the science room door into the hallway. Her face was red, her eyes, tiny pinpricks of anger.

"He's gone, Adrienne! Gone!"

"Who's gone, Jill?" Adrienne was growing tired of Jill's dramatics. She felt the irritation gnawing at her patience. They'd worked for days on their biology display. Jill would have been more help had she stayed home sick.

They'd dissected PorkChop, the earthworm and the other creatures and pinned labels on all the pertinent parts. Rather, Adrienne had dissected, Jill had closed her eyes and poked pins into the specimens, and Adrienne had corrected Jill's bad aim. Adrienne's temper was wearing thin.

"PorkChop is gone!"

"He can't be. You just looked on the wrong shelf. Try the second one from the top, right hand side. I put him away myself yesterday afternoon."

"I looked there, Adrienne."

"So look again. Where would he go?"

"He's gone, I tell you. Gone," Jill moaned and trudged back toward the cooler.

Adrienne heard a yelp from behind the refrigerated wall. Then Jill bolted back into the science lab.

"I told you so! I told you! Here's proof!" Jill was waving a scrap of paper.

"What is it?"

"A ransom note. PorkChop's been kidnapped."

"Give me that," Adrienne grabbed the paper from Jill's fingers. Now she'd seen everything.

The words were cut from old magazines and pasted on the page to make a message. Adrienne felt as if she'd fallen asleep and awakened in the middle of a bad movie.

To Whom It May Concern:

Your pig has been kidnapped. You will only see him safely returned to you if you hand over the last three weeks' biology notes. Leave them in the janitor's room tonight. If you do not do this, you will never see your pig alive.

The Pigsnatchers

P.S. Also leave two Hershey candy bars and two Cokes. Thanks.

"This is ridiculous!"

"Of course it is," Jill pointed out, logical for the first time in days. "PorkChop hasn't been alive for months. How can they return him alive now?"

"Not that! This dumb stunt. Who's goofy enough to kidnap a dead pig?"

"Someone who didn't know how much work we'd put in to this project?" Jill offered. Her eyes looked teary.

Adrienne flung an arm around her friend's shoulder. "Obviously. I have a feeling that we're the latest victims of the senior class, Jill."

Jill nodded morosely. The seniors had been playing outrageous practical jokes on each other and other grades for the past two years. This was just the kind of stunt one of them would pull, trying to outdo the last trickster.

One evening they'd snuck into the lunchroom and set all the tables with dishes—salad and soup bowls, dessert plates, extra silverware. Unfortunately, the janitor and cooks had to unset the tables before anyone could pick up their food in the cafeteria style kitchen.

Another day, the students had come to school to find all the bulletin boards hung upside down. Adrienne thought back to the day Melvin the snake had been released. It was all part of the same nonsense, she was sure. It had been funny until it was *her* project that disappeared.

"What are we going to do?" Jill's lower lip trembled.

Adrienne squared her shoulders inside the oversized turquoise shirt she wore. "Start over."

"Start over?" Jill wailed. "How can we do that?"

"I'm sure Mr. Palley will issue us another pig. We'll just have to stay after school and get it dissected."

"Couldn't we give them the biology notes and the food?" Jill suggested hopefully.

"You know that won't help. PorkChop's a goner. They'd never return him for fear of getting caught. Maybe we can get Mr. Palley to put a lock on the door of the cooler. It won't be so bad."

"Bad. It's going to be awful. I thought I was almost done with this horrible project. How are we going to get the display done by Friday and still have time to work on the decorations for the Fall Fest?"

Adrienne thumped the heel of her hand against her forehead. She could feel her spikey, gelled bangs under her palm. The Fall Fest! How could she have forgotten! It was the most important youth activity at her church. All the intrigue over the Wilsons and PorkChop had made her forget her offer to help Jill decorate the church basement.

"We're going to have to work fast. I can stay late tonight. How about you?"

"Do I have a choice?" Jill pouted.

"Not a chance."

Jill was still pouting two hours later as she and Adrienne prepared to begin work on PorkChop II.

"My brother is going to be mad when he finds out that he has to come and pick me up. He hates it when I have to stay after school."

"My dad isn't going to be very crazy about it either," Adrienne agreed. "Especially when he hears that in order to get both display done and the church decorated before the Fall Fest, I'll have to stay after every night this week."

"Do I hear damsels in distress in here?" Kyle sauntered into the biology room, a stack of textbooks under his arm.

"He's doing it again, Adrienne," Jill complained, "talking like that."

Kyle grinned. That smile made Adrienne's mood soar. He'd been so much more cheerful and friendly lately—to everyone. Maybe all Kyle had needed was someone to pull him out of his shell—and remind him about his vocabulary.

"Let me rephrase that," he grinned. "Are you girls in trouble?"

"That's better," Jill acknowledged. "And yes, yes, yes—we're in big trouble."

"What happened?" He dropped the books to the top of a lab table and turned toward the tray on which they were working. "Hey! What happened to Pork-Chop?"

Silently Adrienne handed him the note.

"Kidnapping a pig? Now these guys have gone too far. Melvin was one thing, but this . . ."

"I suppose it sounds funny if you haven't been working on the project," Adrienne murmured. "I'd bet anything whoever took PorkChop didn't even think about how much work we'd done. The tags that marked the internal organs took two days to make."

"Calligraphy," Jill explained. "I did that."

"I'm really sorry," Kyle looked distressed. "I really am."

"That's okay," Adrienne assured him, not feeling okay at all. "What are you doing here after school?"

"Wrapping up my report. Are you two going to need a ride home?"

Adrienne brightened immediately. "Would you mind? Then my dad could save at least one trip this week."

"Sure. How about you, Jill?"

"Nah. I'll call my grumpy brother. I don't care if he saves a trip. No matter how much he complains, he really likes to come to town and drive up and down main street."

"It's just you and me, then, Adrienne." Kyle smiled at her in a way that made everything around her disappear. Only Jill refused to vanish, instead she persisted in chattering about the church's Fall Fest.

". . . do you think that will be enough construction paper? We can cut two or three leaves out of one sheet. Red, gold and orange ones. To match the streamers. At least we can start with that. I can only cut so long without having my hand feel like it's going to fall off anyway. Does your mother have any gourds or pumpkins in her garden? Adrienne? Adrienne? Are you listening to me?"

Adrienne shook her head. "Uh-huh. Gourds. Red, gold and orange ones. Right?"

Jill gave her friend a disgusted look. "It's a good thing I'm chairman of this committee. You're off in space somewhere. You might be good at biology, but you're hopeless at decorating."

Adrienne waved a hand in the air. "Bring in some hay bales and checkered table cloths. Then everyone can wear jeans and relax."

"Hay bales? Good idea! I'm going to call Pastor Bob right now and ask him if it's all right." Jill scurried from the room before Adrienne could stop her.

"She always thinks up an excuse to get away from this display project," Adrienne explained.

Kyle nodded. "You're probably better off alone. How about if I help you? I'm almost done with my stuff anyway."

A warm glow of pleasure rushed through Adrienne. It was wonderful to be standing next to Kyle, having him help her. He was much more adept at dissection than she, and it seemed like no time until they were relegating PorkChop II to the cooler.

"Thanks. Thanks a lot."

"Anytime."

"Can I help you with your report? As repayment, I mean." Adrienne felt a little embarrassed. Kyle had cut her job in half this afternoon. She would like very much to repay him in some way.

"It's almost done. But, thanks anyway."

The room became quiet. Adrienne could hear the faint hum of the Seth Thomas clock on the wall. At the back of the room, some fish tanks burbled. She shuffled her feet.

Kyle pushed the top book in the pile of texts back and forth between his palms.

Adrienne fingered the wildly colored ceramic parrot she'd pinned to her collar.

Kyle shuffled his feet.

She searched frantically in her brain for something to say, some way to repay him.

Adrienne snapped her fingers. "I've got it!"

"Got what?" Kyle looked startled.

"How I can repay you for helping me—with PorkChop II, for going into the woods with us and . . . everything. . . ." Her voice trailed away.

"How?" Kyle grinned as though he thought she were funny.

"By inviting you to the Fall Fest at church!"

Suddenly Kyle was serious. "You mean it?"

"Sure. Why wouldn't I?"

"I don't know. I've always wondered about it, but I never asked because I didn't want Pastor Bob to think I was, well, hinting for an invitation." Kyle seemed suddenly unsure of himself.

"You don't need to have Pastor Bob's permission to come!" Adrienne blurted. "It's for everyone."

"Maybe . . ."

"No. For sure." Adrienne paused for a moment to gather her thoughts before saying more. "Kyle, would you like to be my guest at the Fall Fest? Everyone gets to bring a friend. I'd like it very much if you'd be mine."

Kyle grinned. "Thanks. I'd like to."

Adrienne could have jumped up and down with glee.

"Now you'd better tell me what to expect." Kyle's voice brought her back to earth.

"Music. Lots of music. Sing-a-longs with guitars. Bible studies. Good food. Games. Races. Usually a scavenger hunt. Bible trivia games. More food. And the very last thing is a campfire. We roast marshmallows and sing. It's a really special day for all the kids from church. Pastor Bob calls it 'fun and fellowship' and I guess that describes it best."

"Sounds nice."

"Kyle?" Adrienne heard the nervous catch in her voice.

"Hmmm?"

"Will your parents mind if you come?"

His expression darkened. "Not if I don't tell them."

"You wouldn't do that, would you?"

"No, probably not." He sighed. "They'll make fun

of it for a while, but they'll let me go. They don't understand how I can be interested in 'hocus-pocus.' "

"But it's not—"

"*I* know that. And *you* know that. But they don't."

Adrienne became quiet and thoughtful. How would she feel if her parents didn't believe in God and she did? It was a disturbing question. Would she be strong enough to stand up to them, to proclaim her faith? When she turned back to Kyle, there was new respect in her eyes.

Before she could express the admiration she was feeling, Jill burst into the room.

"I've got hay bales, I've got saddles, I've got fence posts. Now we can make the Fall Fest have a Western theme and use the leaves and streamers for the dining room only. Great idea, Adrienne! Maybe you *could* be a decorator after all."

"No thanks," Adrienne grinned. "I'm going to stick with becoming a doctor." *Unless*, and she glanced at Kyle, remembering the cabin in the woods and the mysterious Wilsons, *I become a private detective instead.*

There was no time for sleuthing the rest of the week, however.

Jill had everyone within recruiting range working on the Fall Fest.

Even Kyle was getting into the act.

"Jill, you've got enough hay bales in here to winter a herd of cattle. Can't we quit now?"

"Do you really think it's enough?" Jill tapped the eraser of her pencil against her braces. "People are going to use them for benches, you know."

"They aren't supposed to be spending that much time sitting down," Adrienne offered. "They're supposed to be milling around, eating, playing games, singing."

"We have to have some place to break into small groups for Bible studies," Jill insisted. "They're going to have to sit down then."

"Whatever happened to floors and folding chairs?" Kyle asked as he brushed a lock of damp blond hair away from his forehead. Once Jill discovered he was coming to the Fall Fest and was willing to help, she hadn't given him a moment's rest.

Adrienne scanned Kyle's perspiration soaked shirt. His well-developed muscles were not only nice to look at, but a definite asset when trying to unload a pickup load of hay bales.

"Well, let's bring in the fence posts and the saddles next. Once Adrienne gets those fall leaves cut we can decorate the kitchen," Jill announced, more as an order than a suggestion.

Adrienne eyed her friend churlishly. Jill acted as though she were dictator in a country preparing for war.

Adrienne had been cutting leaves out of construction paper for three hours. Her thumb and forefinger had a painful red ring from the child's scissors Jill had provided. Adrienne dropped the instrument to the table with a clatter and sat staring across the church basement.

The Fall Fest would be fun anyway. It always was. It would be especially so, she thought, because Kyle was going to be a part of it.

He'd said little about his parents' response to his request to spend next Sunday at the church. In fact, he'd been unusually quiet on the subject.

Lost in her thoughts, Adrienne jumped when Kyle stepped into her line of vision.

"I'd like to say 'a penny for your thoughts,' but you look so serious that I'd probably have to fork over a dollar."

Adrienne smiled and stretched. The floppy pink

sweater she was wearing slid off her shoulder to reveal a bright green tee-shirt beneath.

"I was thinking about you, actually."

"Me? Should I be flattered or worried?"

"I don't know. I was wondering how your parents took the news that you were going to come to the Fall Fest."

The blue of Kyle's eyes clouded. "Not well."

"Were they angry?"

"No. Church isn't important enough for them to get angry over it. They . . . laughed."

"Laughed?" That seemed worse than anger, somehow. At least anger made it seem like a person *cared*.

"I know. Sounds bad, doesn't it? They think I'm wasting my time." He smiled ruefully. "Then they figured I was doing it because of a girl."

"Me?" Adrienne's voice came out in a squeak.

Kyle nodded. "And I am—partly. Anyway, it's easier for my folks to understand my being interested in a girl than in religion."

"Should *I* be flattered or worried?" Adrienne came back.

Kyle grinned and chucked her under the chin. "Both. Be flattered because I think you're a great girl, Adrienne Fuller. And," he paused, "be worried about my folks. I know I am."

"Have you prayed about it?"

"Best I can. I'm a real novice at this."

"Huh?"

"I'm a beginner. A baby Christian. That's what Pastor Bob calls it."

"That doesn't matter," Adrienne assured him. "God listens anyway. And I'll pray too."

"Thanks." The smile he gave her was warm and gentle and wise. With a start, Adrienne realized that it had been a long time since she'd thought of him as

"The Brain." Now he was just her wonderful friend Kyle.

Before they could continue, Jill, with straw in her hair and a fence post over her shoulder, interrupted them.

"Come *on* you two! Time's a wasting!"

Somehow, by a stroke of genius and ten strokes of good luck, the preparations for Fall Fest were ready by Saturday night.

Adrienne and Kyle stopped at the church on their way home from the Science Fair.

Kyle flopped down onto a hay bale and leaned his head against the wall.

"Whew! What a day."

"You can say that again." Adrienne, wearing black pants and a fuschia sweatshirt, plopped down beside him. Then her eyes began to twinkle. "I think we did all right for ourselves, don't you?"

Kyle didn't open his eyes, but a wide grin split his even features. "Sure did." His eyelids fluttered. "First place overall, Kyle Rogers."

"*And* the judges took the time to look me up and compliment me on the display in the science room!"

"And they wrote down your name . . ."

"And told Mr. Palley they'd like to make a comment for my record . . ."

"And Jill is going to get a passing grade for this quarter . . ."

"And maybe even a *good* grade . . ."

". . . because Mr. Palley said she went 'above and beyond' in effort."

"But she has to keep up the good work for the next three quarters . . ."

"And if she does . . ."

". . . she might get a chance at being a lab assistant next year in biology!"

With that the two of them broke into uproarious laughter.

"Can't you see it?" Adrienne giggled, wiping away tears of mirth. "*Jill Wainwright*, biology assistant?"

"She'll have the classroom redecorated in no time!"

Kyle and Adrienne looked at each other and hooted. When their laughter subsided, they sank into a companionable silence.

It had been a good day. A wonderful day. For nearly a week, Adrienne had been able to put Ted and little Jeffrey out of her mind. But now, in the quiet dimness of the decorated church basement, thoughts of them returned.

What had Ted and Jeffrey done for fun today? Stayed shuttered and fearful in the cabin while their father patrolled the woods? And what would they be doing tomorrow while she and Kyle and Jill were having fun with their friends? Staying alone again, afraid to peek through the darkened windows?

Whatever was going on with the Wilsons was nagging at her again. Adrienne rubbed the palms of her hands against the tops of her thighs. Tomorrow she would concentrate on the Fall Fest, but after school on Monday she knew her mind would return to the lonely, frightened family in the woods.

Chapter Seven

A nervous tickle danced in Adrienne's stomach as she waited on the front porch for Kyle to pick her up. She'd rushed home from church to get ready for the Fall Fest which started with a noon luncheon. The food was traditional—barbecued beef on buns, potato chips, jello with whipped cream, brownies. Adrienne licked her lips in anticipation of her favorite foods.

She smoothed a hand across her denim skirt. It wasn't often, other than Sunday mornings, that Adrienne relented and wore a dress, but this was a really wonderful outfit and she'd been anxious to wear it.

The skirt was straight and narrow, stone-washed denim with lots of top-stitching and decorative copper rivets and snaps. The hem grazed the tops of her cowboy boots. The jacket was oversized and lined with a red plaid flannel that matched her shirt.

The whistle that came floating across that farmyard assured her that her fashion sense was on target.

"Awright!" Kyle yelled as he pulled in front of the house. "You look great."

"Not bad yourself," Adrienne returned. He was wearing denim too and a soft blue Western shirt that made his blue eyes wider and more intense than ever.

"I'm feeling a little awkward," he admitted as they

pulled from the Fuller yard. "Maybe I'll be out of place. After all, I don't exactly belong to your church. I've only gone once."

"Give our youth group exactly ten minutes to make you feel comfortable," Adrienne suggested confidently. "Then decide if you're out of place or not."

It didn't even take five minutes before Kyle was surrounded by people welcoming him. At ten minutes after the hour, he winked at Adrienne. "You were right—again."

Adrienne grinned. These were people she could count on to show caring concern and friendship. Kyle might have a high IQ, but he'd certainly missed out in other areas. Maybe today would show him just how important having a church home was.

"If I eat another s'more I'm going to explode," Jill groaned. It was nearing ten o'clock and people were beginning to drift out of the church parking lot where they'd built a bonfire for the marshmallow roast.

"That would be more interesting than fireworks," Adrienne commented, too full to stand up and leave.

"Don't tell me there are still fireworks to come," Kyle groaned. "I have to go home. If I can get up, that is."

"No fireworks. Unless Jill *does* explode," Adrienne responded. "And next year I think the food committee can cut down a little."

"Like about fifty percent."

"At least."

"We didn't have to finish it all just because it was there."

"I hate to see anything go to waste," Adrienne groaned, regretting the last two s'mores and three barbecues she'd had for supper.

"Now its going to go to *waist* instead!" Jill chirruped. "Get it? Go to *waste* and go to waist? Get it?"

"Yes, Jill, we got it," Kyle and Adrienne chimed in unison. "But we don't want it."

"Harumph." Jill scrambled to her feet. "I've got to go. Clean up is tomorrow at three thirty. See you in school."

Kyle and Adrienne exchanged a glance. Their big weekend was over. The Science Fair and the Fall Fest were history now. What was next for them?

What was next? The question came to Adrienne as she wandered into the Fuller's empty kitchen late Monday afternoon. She felt purposeless and let down. The projects she'd worked so hard for were completed. What should she do next?

Her eyes fell on a scrap of note paper on the counter.

> Adrienne—Go to the cabin and check on the firewood. If it's really low, I'll take an entire rick up there on the truck.
>
> Dad

Adrienne felt a surge of energy flow through her. The cabin! Of course! *That's* what was next. She'd been so involved with her own life that she'd forgotten the Wilsons for a moment, the poachers, the woods. Suddenly, she was eager to be on her way.

The woods were silent. Autumn always seemed a quieter time to Adrienne. Spring made the forest fairly crackle with activity, but in fall the sounds and movements of the woods seemed slower, dimmer, more nearly silent.

As she walked through the trees in their red and gold garb, she wondered if her imagination had run away with her where the Wilsons were concerned.

The poaching reports had moved out of this area somewhat. No carcasses or entrails had been found on her father's farm in some time. Either Wilson had become more cautious or he was not a poacher at all.

Adrienne wanted to believe the second theory. She wanted Wilson and his connection with the poachers to be a product of her overactive imagination. For Ted's sake. And for Jeffrey's.

The cabin looked deserted. The Wilsons had allowed weeds to grow around the base of the house. A broken tree limb lay over the pathway to the door.

Staying in the shelter of the trees, Adrienne made her way toward the side of the cabin to check the woodpile.

Most of the wood was gone.

That meant the Wilsons had built a fire almost every evening. Adrienne was glad for that. She didn't like the idea of Jeffrey being cold. She made her way back over the trail she had followed until she was standing in front of the cabin, just shy of the clearing. She could see the front door but, standing as she was, she knew she was invisible from inside the house.

For a moment, she just stood there and stared. She was so convinced that the cabin was empty, that when Jeffrey's face peered out the window, she had to stifle a gasp.

The little boy's head rose over the sill in the same manner as the last time she'd seen him in the window. His mouth was puckered into a silent O and he stared intently into the trees.

He was looking for his daddy. Adrienne could sense it in the way the child scanned the paths that led from the cabin into the woods. Mutely, he pushed his nose toward the glass until his entire face was pressed against the rain-spattered window.

Silently, Adrienne backed away. She didn't want to be there when Ed Wilson came home. Jeffrey might be looking forward to seeing him, but she wasn't. Not in the least.

Mechanically, Adrienne followed the trail homeward. Her mind was intently traveling another path.

What if Jeffrey's father really *was* a poacher like she suspected? Should she report her suspicions to her father? To the game warden? What if he were caught and sent to jail? What would happen to Ted and Jeffrey then?

She mulled the questions over and over in her mind all the way home. She didn't want Mr. Wilson to be a criminal. Not at all. This time Adrienne *wanted* to be wrong. To be way off-base. But Wilson's mysterious behavior led her to believe otherwise.

Did *she* want to be the one to actually discover that Mr. Wilson was on the wrong side of the law? A criminal? A poacher? Where was her responsibility? With the law? Or with Ted and Jeffrey?

It was a bigger problem than she'd ever faced before. Silently, she prayed for guidance.

Feeling slightly better, assured that now she had some divine help with her problem, Adrienne made her way into the house.

"Adrienne, Kyle is here!"

Adrienne groaned and rolled to the edge of her bed.

Her head hurt. She couldn't get the picture of Jeffrey in the cabin window, his face pressed forlornly against the glass, out of her thoughts. All evening she'd been trying to sort out the imaginary from the facts. What clues did they really have that Ed Wilson was anything more than he said he was? None. Except . . . and the whirling questions started again.

"Hi. You look awful." Kyle was standing at the bottom of the stairs.

"Thanks a bunch. I needed that."

"Sorry. But you do."

"I suppose so."

"What's going on?"

Adrienne appreciated the concerned look on Kyle's face. "Come on. Let's go onto the porch and I'll tell you." She scuffled out to the screened enclosure with dragging feet.

Kyle swung one long leg across a folding chair and sat down in it backwards, his legs straddling the cushioned back. "So tell me, what's wrong?"

"Something's bothering me."

"Obviously."

"Don't use any bigger words than that on me or I'll clam up," Adrienne warned. She was in no mood for challenges.

"Promise."

"I don't know what to do about the Wilsons."

"What are you supposed to do?"

"Nothing, really. I just keep thinking that if he's a poacher and I don't say so, I'm guilty of something, too."

"But do you have any proof—real proof—that he *is* a poacher?"

"No."

"So why worry?"

"But what if he is? And what about Ted and Jeffrey? Why are they locked up in that cabin all day? I know they are. I saw the little guy peeking out the window again today. Something is wrong up there, Kyle, and I don't know whom to talk to about it."

"Maybe before you go getting anybody upset and making a fool of yourself, you should be sure something is going on. Not everyone is the same, Adrienne. Maybe those people just like their privacy."

"I've thought of that. And I keep thinking that I've got a serious case of over-active-imagination-itis. I feel this . . . this . . ." and her eyes began to twinkle, "this *urgency*."

"Wow! Big word! Talk so I can understand you, Fuller!" Kyle whooped, poking her in the shoulder with his fist.

Adrienne ducked her head and grinned. "Sometimes even we 'average' students can use an above average word, you know."

Kyle was thoughtful for a moment. Then he murmured softly, "I can't think of a single way in which you're average, Adrienne, not a one."

Feeling more lighthearted and much better than she had before Kyle's arrival, Adrienne stood up and brushed the seat of her pants with her hands. "Well, I do make an 'extra-ordinary' batch of popcorn. Want some?"

"You bet." Together they wound their way back to the kitchen.

Adrienne couldn't sleep. Her pillow was too flat on one end and too fat on the other. Her mattress had developed a new lump and a matching dip. She flip-flopped from side to side like a fish out of water. Every time she closed her eyes she thought of Ted and Jeffrey and of Mr. Wilson. By morning, Adrienne felt as though she'd run a marathon race—at least twelve times over.

"You look tired, dear. Didn't you sleep well?" Naomi Fuller brushed a concerned hand across Adrienne's forehead.

"Not very."

"Your eyes have purplish shadows beneath them. Are you sure you're not ill?"

"I'm fine. I just had lots on my mind."

"I know the feeling," Wayne Fuller interjected. "I have to get to the bank the minute it opens. I just discovered that the insurance on the car has lapsed. I have to get the policy renewed before your mother has an accident."

"Me? Wayne, I'm the most careful driver on earth," Naomi protested.

"Sure you are. That's why we have dents in both fenders."

"That wasn't my fault, Wayne. That grocery store parking lot is just a very dangerous place—oh! That reminds me! I promised to get groceries for Mrs. Swanson. Ever since she broke her leg she's been having such a time. . . . Can I ride with you?"

"Safer than having you drive," Adrienne's father commented. "Let's go right now. I'll take you out for breakfast. How about it, Adrienne? Want to join us?"

"Thanks, Dad, but I think I'll just wait for the school bus. All I want is a bowl of cereal anyway. I've got a couple of poems left to read for English class."

"Suit yourself. Have a good day."

Adrienne watched her parents climb into the family car. She gave a big yawn and a cat-like stretch. Her stomach was growling. Adrienne rubbed her midsection and headed for the cupboards. Cheerios. Cereal bowl. Sugar bowl. Milk. It was the last carton, too. She hoped her mother would remember to buy groceries for them as well.

She poured her cereal and milk into the bowl. Sleepily, she tried to sink the bobbing little circles in the milk, but they bounced to the top again.

"Wish *I* had some extra bounce today," Adrienne announced to the world in general. She ate a few spoonfuls of cereal before finding herself staring off into space. Idly, she poked at the milk carton with her spoon.

"Grade A, pasturized, homogenized, Vitamin A & D," she read aloud. "Serving size—one cup. . . ." She poked at the carton again, bringing another side into view.

"Have you seen these children?" she read. The final syllables stuck in her throat.

Three postage stamp sized photos were printed on the waxy carton. Two girls and a boy. A familiar boy. Jeffrey Wilson's face was staring at her from the back of the milk carton on her breakfast table.

But it wasn't Jeffrey. At least the *name* on the carton wasn't Jeffrey Wilson. It was Jeffrey Conrad. Age at time of disappearance—three. Height—36 inches. Weight—39 pounds. Hair color—brown. Eyes—blue. Date of disappearance—August.

Jeffrey Wilson and Jeffrey Conrad were the same child!

Adrienne's hands were shaking as she lowered her spoon to the bowl. What was she going to do now?

Her eyes flew back to the carton. It was still there, the image of little Jeffrey, pressed in wax, hazy yet recognizable.

Missing! Adrienne's mouth went dry. She'd known something was wrong at the cabin, but this! If only her parents were home! She pushed herself away from the table. She would call them, tell them that there was an emergency. . . .

Adrienne's fingers trembled over the telephone dial. She didn't know where they'd gone! It could be any one of a dozen places.

She heard a telltale crunch on the driveway.

The school bus! Hurriedly, Adrienne poured the remaining milk from the carton. She put the container into her school bag. Kyle would know what to do if that really was Jeffrey Wilson on the carton.

Kyle was sitting in the back seat of the bus, studying. Jill was in the seat in front of him combing her hair. Adrienne's feet felt leaden as she made her way toward the back. Thankfully, there were several empty seats this morning, most of them at the rear. At least they could talk in private.

"Hi. Did you get those poems read?" Jill put away her mirror and comb. "*Boring!* Who cares about that stuff, anyway? I like poems that rhyme best. Anybody can write that other stuff. Why, I bet—Adrienne, are you listening to me?"

"Huh? Oh, sorry, Jill. I've got something on my mind."

"You must. You look spaced out. What's wrong?"

Kyle had laid his book on the seat. Now he leaned forward as Adrienne sat down beside Jill. "Adrienne? You'd better tell us what's happened."

Silently, Adrienne pulled the milk carton from her bag and handed it to him.

"What's this about, Fuller? Another PorkChop project? If you think you're going to get me involved . . ." Jill's chatter ground to a halt at the expression on Kyle's face. He handed her the carton.

"Oh, boy." Jill stared openmouthed at the picture. Then she gave nervous little giggle. "Funny, isn't it, how much kids resemble each other. If that picture weren't so fuzzy you could even think it was . . ." Her eyes widened. "You mean it might be—"

"It's an awfully good resemblance," Adrienne pointed out. "The age and size aren't too far off."

"It's not a good picture," Kyle put in. "I'm sure there are other little kids that . . ." His voice drained away. "*Maybe* there are other kids that . . ."

"What are we going to do, Kyle?" Adrienne's voice was nearly a wail.

"I guess we'd better tell someone."

"Who?" Jill questioned. Her eyes were wide as Frisbees.

"No!" Adrienne protested. "Not yet!"

"What?" Kyle and Jill's voices chimed together. "Why not?"

Adrienne chewed at her lower lip. "I've got to be sure first. Absolutely and positively sure. I've got to go to the cabin and take another look at Jeffrey."

"Are you crazy?"

"No. The little boy looks a lot like Jeffrey Wilson, but you know how it is. Maybe if I saw Jeffrey again I'd realize that it wasn't the same child at all. I can't go having my dad report that the people who rent our cabin are . . . kidnappers."

"They can't really be kidnappers anyway, can they?" Jill asked.

"What do you mean?"

"Well, Jeffrey sure looks like his dad to me. How could a kidnapper manage that? And he doesn't seem afraid of his father either. And Ted's too young to . . ." Jill paused and scratched her head. "I think I'm all mixed up."

"Me too," Adrienne admitted. "That's why I have to go to the cabin *one more time.* I have to be sure."

"You can't go up there! Not now. Not now that we know Wilson might be a kidnapper," Jill protested.

Adrienne clapped a hand over her friend's mouth. "Not so loud. Anyway, we were up there before and he didn't hurt us. If he doesn't think we know anything, there's no reason for him to bother us. If he didn't before, he won't now."

"I'm not so sure about that," Jill maintained. "I think you're crazy to try it."

"I'm afraid I do too, Adrienne," Kyle put in. "You might get hurt."

"I'll be careful," Adrienne assured him. "But I have to go."

"You can't go alone." Kyle's voice was firm and commanding.

"But I can't tell my dad. Not yet. I'll have to—"

"I'll go with you then."

"You would? You'd do that for me?" Adrienne's eyes were round with wonder.

"I can't let you go stomping off into the woods now that we know that Wilson might be a kidnapper. If he took Jeffrey—or Ted—he wouldn't hesitate to take you. Anyway," and Kyle mockingly flexed his muscles, "The Brain's got muscles too."

"What about me?"

"You?" Kyle and Adrienne chimed together. They'd almost forgotten Jill.

"Yes me. I'm part of this group, you know," Jill announced huffily. "Or have you already forgotten?"

"I didn't think you'd want to go back to the cabin, Jill. I thought you'd be . . ." Adrienne let her voice trail away.

"Scared? You thought I'd be scared?" Jill wrinkled her nose. "You bet I'll be scared—but that's no worse than being left out!"

Kyle gave a big laugh and lightly slapped Jill on the back. "Good girl! The intrepid Jill Wainright strikes again!"

"Huh?"

Kyle had the grace to look foolish. "The *brave* Jill Wainright strikes again."

"That's better."

"This vocabulary lesson is getting us nowhere," Adrienne groused. "What about the cabin. Can we go tonight?"

"After school," Kyle announced. "We're going in and out again as fast as we can. You can get *one look* at Jeffrey to satisfy yourself that it's really him on the milk carton. Then we're going to get your dad and go to the police. *One look*, Adrienne. That's all."

"What excuse can I use to get inside?" Adrienne's stomach was doing nervous flip-flops. She liked Ted and Jeffrey. Doing something so sneaky—something that could end up helping them or hurting them— made her feel all weak and quivery inside.

"Does your mother usually take anything up to the cabin—supplies, food, that sort of thing?"

"Not food. But she does change the light bulbs and bring up any old appliances once we get new ones at the house. She said she would take the old toaster up when—that's it! The toaster! I'll bring it and some light bulbs. That should be good enough."

"It had better be," Kyle muttered grimly. It was obvious that he didn't like this operation one bit. Adrienne was afraid he might want to back out.

"We'll just drop it off and go right back to our farm, Kyle. Honest. Why would I want to hang around up there any longer than I have to? But I have to be sure, Kyle. What if this photo is all a big mistake? If we report it without being positive, we could cause a lot of trouble for the Wilsons."

Unwillingly, Kyle nodded. "I don't know why I'm letting you talk me into this, Fuller, but remember, only one look. We'll meet at your place after school. We'll have to hurry. It's starting to get dark awfully early these days. Deal?"

Adrienne and Jill chimed after him, "Deal."

It was already darker in the woods than Adrienne liked. Darkness came earlier in the fall, already dusk was fast approaching.

"We've got to hurry," Adrienne hissed. "I don't want to be out here after dark."

"You can say that again," Jill agreed. "It's getting cold." She had her hands tucked into the kangaroo pocket of her sweatshirt and its hood tied securely around her face. Her skin was pale with nervousness. Jill seemed to be all eyes and braces.

Adrienne, having read too many mystery books, had decided to dress in black. Only her flame red hair made her apparent in the heavy shadows of the brush. Kyle was restlessly shifting from foot to foot, waiting for the girls.

"It's spooky tonight," Jill complained.

"It's no different than a hundred other nights. What's different is what you're thinking about," Adrienne pointed out.

A twig snapped beneath her feet. Adrienne jumped. Maybe Jill was right. It *was* spooky out tonight. Only Kyle's big, warm and silent presence made her feel secure. Gratefully, she turned to look at him.

"I'm glad you're here."

"I'm glad *you're* glad." He didn't sound happy. He didn't look happy either. His expression was grim as they trekked through the woods.

The cabin seemed farther away than usual tonight. Or perhaps Adrienne was moving more slowly, dreading what she might find there.

A low-hanging branch scraped bony fingers across her shoulder. Adrienne shuddered.

A cloud skudded across the sky above them, casting a pall in the already dimming light. A trickle of fear crept down Adrienne's spine.

A rabbit scurried in front of her. Adrienne stifled a gasp. What was wrong with her tonight, anyway? This was her home, the forest in which she'd grown up, the trails she and her father had made.

Adrienne paused to cock her head and listen. Her friends slowed. Silence. Again Adrienne started walking. She could hear the crunch of leaves and twigs beneath her feet.

Jill and Kyle's soft footsteps moved behind her. Adrienne relaxed a bit. There were the familiar noises of the forest surrounding her. There were the faint and muted sounds of her friends behind her. There was the murmur of a voice ahead of her. . . .

She stopped abruptly. Voices? Now? Whose? And why?

Chapter Eight

Adrienne held out her hand to stop Jill and Kyle. Her fingers grazed the fleecy pocket of Jill's sweater.

"What's—" Jill began, but Adrienne waved her into silence. The three sets of footsteps ceased. Adrienne pointed to the small clearing to her right.

Three men in thick, soiled jackets and dirty boots occupied the clearing. Two stood, bent at the shoulders, their heads and necks obscured by upturned collars and battered hats pulled low over their eyes. The third, dressed in army fatigues, knelt on the ground over the carcass of a newly felled deer.

His knife danced over the body, slicing a gash down the center of the fallen creature's belly. Adrienne could see the glassy glint of the creature's unclosed, dead eyes.

The man paused to drink from a canteen near his feet.

"This one's a beaut, ain't he?" The voice of the one in army fatigues carried across the clearing to where the three youngsters were huddled.

"Big 'un, that's fer sure. It's gonna be some work to dress this one out."

"You ain't skeered of work, are ya, Hank?"

Hank, the taller of the two men standing, threw

back his head and laughed. Adrienne could see a row of yellow, rotted teeth in a pink, wet mouth. "Me? Skeered of work? 'Course not, Milt. Why else would I have a high-powered fancy job like this one?" He tittered nervously, his laugh grating on Adrienne's nerves like fingernails on a chalkboard, raising the fine, small hairs at the base of her neck.

In those first moments, she tried to remember everything about the three men. Her father and the game warden would need to know. Hank was tall and thin, "Stringbean" would be a good name for him. And she would never forget the ugly slash of his smile.

Milt was shorter and rounder. His stomach hung over his belt and outside the tattered denim jacket he wore, straining at the confines of a dirty shirt with tomato stains on its front. His hair was brown and greasy, spiking from beneath the circle of a blue and gray cap.

The third man, bending over the deer, was obviously younger than the other two. Adrienne could tell by the square of his shoulders and the easy way he moved as he gutted the deer. Though she couldn't see his face, she guessed him to be not much older than twenty-five.

Her gaze returned to the other men. They were probably in their forties—about the same age as her father or as . . . and she gave a small gasp . . . as Mr. Wilson.

So Wilson wasn't a poacher after all! But, Adrienne shivered as she remembered the picture on the milk carton; he was something much, much worse.

Adrienne could feel Jill tugging at the back of her jacket. Kyle's hand snaked around her shoulder. They had to go. Silently, they must back away from this horrid little scene in the clearing and run—run for help, for safety.

"Come on." Kyle's voice was barely a whisper.

Adrienne nodded and turned around. If they could only get a few yards down the trail, they would be safe. These men were too engrossed in their bloody kill and whatever was in that dirty canteen to move quickly away from that spot.

As she turned, Adrienne bumped into Jill. Jill's eyes were dilated and focused on the spot in the clearing. Her mouth worked, but no sound came out. Jill seemed frozen with terror.

"Move it!" Adrienne whispered the order into her friend's ear. "Quietly."

Woodenly, Jill turned, but as she did, her shoulder grazed the branch of an evergreen. What happened next, Adrienne was not quite sure.

Stumbling away from the sharp needles, Jill stepped on the tip of a branch. The dry branch gave a sharp popping sound. It seemed the forest was suddenly alive with their noise.

"Who's there?" It was Hank speaking. He reared up like an angry stallion and headed for the forest.

"Run!"

Adrienne tried. Oh, how she tried. Her feet churned, her lungs burned from lack of oxygen, her eyes watered. But she was not moving. She flailed and scrambled, but Milt held her fast.

"I got one!" he chortled near her ear. Adrienne's stomach turned at the smell of his breath.

"And I got a pair," Hank snarled. He had Kyle by the throat, the boy's head tucked tightly under his arm. Kyle looked as though he was having trouble breathing. Jill followed dazedly behind.

The third man came upon them now, a gun resting casually in the crook of his elbow.

"Well, well, what have we got here?"

"Snoops. That's what."

"Snoops, eh?"

"You kids know what happens to snoops?"

"Let me go!" Adrienne gave a hard backward kick into the shin of her captor.

"Punk!" he screamed back. Without letting her go, he grabbed a chunk of her thick auburn hair and gave it a jerk. Quick, hot tears flowed down her face.

"I told you we shouldn't have been so close to the trail, Carl."

"Shaddup, Hank. We gotta tie these three up while we get these carcasses loaded."

"What are we going to do with them?"

The younger man, the one called Carl, allowed his gaze to rest briefly on each of the three captives. He rolled what was undoubtedly a plug of chewing tobacco around in his mouth, then spat at the ground. "I dunno yet. I haven't thought about it." His eyes narrowed to thin slits. "Tie 'em up."

Hank and Milt jumped to do Carl's bidding. Adrienne's arms were jerked backward around the trunk of a small tree. Jill was whimpering. Adrienne could see tears streaking her small, white face.

They tied Kyle the tightest. Adrienne could tell by the pained grimace on his features when they tugged at the scrap of rope that held him to the tree.

"You kids got in on more than you bargained for this time," Carl growled. He was barely twenty-five, Adrienne guessed. Though clean-shaven and the cleanest of the trio, Adrienne was most afraid of him.

It was his eyes. Gray and glassy, they glittered with some sort of frightening, cruel light. Adrienne wondered if that was what insanity looked like in a man's eyes.

The thought washed over her in a flood of fear. *Insanity.* They'd been insane to come here, to the forest, but she and her friends were not nearly so mad as these men who butchered innocent, unprotected creatures for a living.

Would they care any more for humans then they did for the forest animals?

"Hurry. We gotta load up. I don't want to leave any of this kill behind. We've gotta get out of here. Too crowded. Too dangerous." Carl barked the orders and Hank and Milt carried them out.

Carl pulled a long, thin knife from the sheath at his waist.

Jill gave a low, terrified moan.

Kyle struggled against the rope that held him fast.

Adrienne prayed.

Carl's low, evil laughter filled the clearing. Slowly, methodically, he wiped the blade on the leg of his pants. Then he drew the knife upward until he held it waist high. With a chuckle, he began to clean the clotted blood from beneath his fingernails.

A wave of relief washed over Adrienne.

What had she expected him to do? Then the realization hit her. Whatever it was she had feared most, he might do yet.

"Gotta go, kids. I'll be back after we get loaded up." Carl bent to pick up a gun and a rain slicker, then he turned and smiled an empty, threatening grimace. "And that's a promise."

"We're dead. We're dead. There's no way out. We're dead," Jill moaned. "I'm too young to die. I haven't even graduated from high school yet. I'll never get to be an interior decorator." She was rolling her head back and forth against the tree. Tears streamed down her cheeks. "I had a fight with my brother this morning. I never got to say I'm sorry. Now I'm going to die and he'll never know that I didn't mean it. . . ."

Adrienne wanted to call out to her friend and comfort her, but something was tugging at her ropes. A soft, hurried voice came from behind her. "Be quiet. It's me, Ted. I'll cut you loose."

A brief sawing noise accompanied the tugging at her wrists and then she was free. Then Ted was thrusting another knife into her hands. "You get Kyle.

I'll do Jill. Then we've got to run to the cabin."

Adrienne nodded. The blood was pumping fast and hard in her veins. Run. Run.

She sawed at Kyle's ropes. His hands were already turning blue from the pressure of the bindings, but he didn't cry out as she freed him. He took a moment to rub his wrists then grabbed her elbow and hissed, "Come on. You lead. You know the woods better than we do."

As they moved soundlessly through the trees, Adrienne scanned the wooded landscape for familiar landmarks. She rarely ventured off the trails anymore, and overgrowth was thick in spots, but unerringly she led the way to the cabin.

The closer they came to the tiny house in the woods, the faster their feet flew. Ted had a key out and ready before they burst through the clearing. His hands trembled at the lock and he gave a gusty sigh of relief when the door swung open.

Jeffrey was standing on the other side.

"Did you come to see us?" The little boy was holding a battered teddy bear under one arm and a soft, well-worn blanket in the other.

"Did you just wake up?" Ted asked his brother. "I thought you'd sleep for a long time yet."

"Not tired."

"Then go put your bear to bed. I think he's tired." Ted ruffled the little boy's hair.

Jeffrey nodded obediently and trotted toward the bedroom. Once he disappeared, the four teenagers sank with shaking knees to chairs and couches around the room.

Kyle was the first to speak. "Where'd you come from, anyway? I was never so glad to see someone in my entire life!"

Ted smiled weakly. "I was behind some shrubs on the other side of the clearing. "I've been watching those guys for almost a week now. I was listening, hoping one of them would say their full names or something about themselves. I'm real quiet on my feet. They never even knew I was there."

"Did you get anything?"

"Not much. They drove a pickup truck, but every time I got close they had it backed into shrubs. I could never get the license number."

"You got a make and the color?"

"Sure, but how many dozen red and white Ford pickups are there in this country?"

"Did they ever say anything about themselves?" Now that Jill was safe, her curiosity was as active as ever.

"From what I can figure out, the older two are brothers. I think the younger guy is the brains and he must be a cousin or something. They've been poaching the woods all fall. I think they did it somewhere else before this. It sounds like they've made lots of money and that's why they've stayed so long in one place. Good pelts."

"No last names?"

"No. Just Hank, Milt and Carl. Carl's the mean one." Ted scratched his head. "He did say he'd been in the army, though. They wore a lot of army fatigues and camouflage clothing."

"It's a start, anyway. Maybe the police will know how to use it to identify those guys," Kyle commented. He was still rubbing at his sore wrists.

"Who says the police are going to find out?" Ted's voice was sharp and harsh.

Three pair of amazed eyes turned to stare at him.

"You can't mean you don't want us to report this!"

"We've got to! Those men could have killed us!"

"We can't let them go. You've seen how many animals they've killed."

Ted bowed his head until his chin rested on his

shirt collar. When he looked up there was a hard and stubborn glint in his eyes. "No."

"But why?" Jill breathed. "If they'd found you, they would have hurt you."

"No. I can't."

"But you've got to have a reason, Ted," Kyle pointed out. "I don't understand why you didn't go to the police as soon as you discovered them poaching."

The boy shrugged. His shoulders looked thin under his shirt. "My dad wants privacy. If I go reporting that the poachers have a camp up here, there will be people stomping all over the woods. That's not what we came up here for. We came here to . . . get away. To have privacy. We don't want all that attention."

His voice rose as he spoke. Each word seemed more determined than the last. "We don't want any publicity."

The room was silent for a moment, then Adrienne spoke.

"Is that because you don't want anyone to find out that Mr. Wilson is a kidnapper?"

If a pin had dropped, it would have sounded like a steel girder falling to the floor.

Ted's eyes grew wide and fearful. "Why would you say something like that about my father?"

"Is he your father, Ted? Really? You can tell us if he's not—if he's holding you here against your will. We've all seen Jeffrey's photo on the "Missing Child" poster. It was on a milk carton. Are you a missing child, too?"

A variety of emotions played across Ted's features. Amazement, horror, fear.

"You've made a mistake."

"I don't think so, Ted. I wanted to come up here today and take another look at Jeffrey just to make sure it *wasn't* a mistake. Now I know. Jeffrey Wilson is really Jeffrey Conrad and he's a missing child."

"No!" The word held more terror than Adrienne had ever heard. The harsh sound grated on her ears, but she persisted.

"If you are in trouble, you need to get help. You helped us. Now we can help you. You don't have to stay here. We can get you both away from Mr. Wilson. My parents can help." Adrienne held out her hand to the trembling boy, "Please?"

Ted would not look at her. Instead, he glanced down and away, ignoring her outstretched hand. Adrienne turned pleading eyes to Kyle, begging for assistance.

But Kyle was not looking at her. Instead, he was staring at the door at the far end of the room which led to the bedroom. Adrienne's glance followed Kyle's gaze.

Mr. Wilson stood in the doorway.

Fear like shards of ice stabbed at her. Jill slumped against her chair.

Not again! They'd jumped from the frying pan directly into the fire. There seemed to be bad men everywhere.

Wilson came toward Adrienne. How much had he heard?

Everything, no doubt. She could tell by the expression on his face. He'd heard it all. Now what would he do?

Adrienne's heart felt like a stone in her chest. She prayed a silent, terrified prayer for it seemed that only a true miracle could help her now.

Wilson raised his arm as he approached her. Adrienne shrank back against her seat. Would he hit her? Worse?

Their legs were almost touching. His pant legs brushed her knees. Adrienne trembled. The hand loomed over her.

Then slowly, gently it came down upon her head

in a caress. Much to Adrienne's dumbfounded amazement, Ed Wilson rested the palm of his hand tenderly
on her flame-red hair.

Idly, he tucked a loose strand of hair behind her
ear. His expression was thoughtful. Adrienne
straightened and dared to gaze into his eyes.

Wilson had tears in his eyes.

Stunned, Adrienne turned toward Kyle. He
shrugged his shoulders in bewilderment.

"Dad?" Ted neared Wilson.

"It's all right, son. It's all right."

"But they want to call the police. They called you
a . . ." The boy's voice caught in his throat.

Ed Wilson eyed the boy for a moment before stat-
ing, "I think we have to tell them, son. It's time to
finally tell the truth."

Just then, when Adrienne thought she would
burst from the tension, Jeffrey toddled into the room.

"Bear's in bed. Sleepy bear." Without hesitation,
the little boy went toward Wilson, tugged on the man's
pant leg and held his arms open wide to be picked up.

Adrienne shook her head in confusion. How could
this man be a kidnapper? These boys seemed to love
him, not fear him.

"Well, son? Do you agree?"

Son. Wilson called Ted son. Then who was the kidnapper?

"I suppose. I don't know how we can keep it a secret now. Not after those poachers . . ."

Wilson nodded. He picked up Jeffrey and carried
him to the couch. Then he turned to the three sitting
rigidly in the chairs. "Hot chocolate and popcorn, anyone? It's a long story that we have to tell."

Much to Adrienne's amazement, he busied himself popping corn and heating milk for the cocoa. No
one spoke except Jeffrey who kept clapping his hands
and cheering, "Corn! Corn! Cocoa and corn!"

When he had prepared two large bowls of popcorn and drizzled them with melted butter and set six mugs of hot chocolate on the table, Wilson sat down beside Jeffrey. The child, all buttery from the small dish of popcorn he had in his fist, climbed into Wilson's lap.

Adrienne and her friends were rooted to their spots.

After a long silence, Wilson began to speak.

"I'm not a kidnapper. Ted and Jeffrey are my sons."

Jeffrey gave a buttery grin and threw his arms around Wilson's neck. "Daddy," he announced proudly. "Jeffrey's daddy."

"Then why did I find Jeffrey's photograph in a "Missing Children" campaign?" Adrienne felt a little of her old feistiness returning. It had been a dreadful, frightening day and she was weary and confused. She needed to make sense of the events occurring around her.

Ed Wilson's shoulders sank and a pale, haunted look masked his face. His voice was full of emotion as he shakily began his story. "I think I'd better start at the beginning."

Chapter Nine

"Ted's mother was my first wife," Mr. Wilson began. He smiled a faint, sad smile. "We were very young and very much in love."

Adrienne felt the hard, critical ideas she'd had about Wilson beginning to dissolve. Jeffrey had curled cozily into his father's arms and was falling asleep. No one could be as evil as she'd first thought and hold a child with that much tenderness.

"We'd been married only two years when Ted was born. My," Mr. Wilson stretched out his long legs and readjusted Jeffrey on his lap, "we were so proud. I don't think there were any two happier people in the world than Melissa and I."

Ted shuffled his feet again, but this time he had a happy, relaxed look across his features.

"He was a good baby, as I remember. Hardly ever cried," Wilson recalled. Ted looked embarrassed.

"Good thing, too."

Adrienne watched the silent communication between the two. It seemed that Wilson was gaining strength to continue from his son.

Wilson shook himself. "Ted's mother died when he was only two."

Jill, Kyle and Adrienne all found themselves glancing sympathetically at the boy. Adrienne moved her chair a little closer to Kyle's. She needed to sense his strength and stability right now.

"We got along pretty well, Ted and I. Didn't we son?"

Ted nodded. "Real good, Dad. Until—" He stopped. An angry flush colored his features.

"Until I married Angela." Wilson sunk again into the sad and thoughtful state that seemed to characterize him so well. "Worst mistake I ever made." Wilson looked down at his tiny, sleeping son. "The only good that came out of our marriage was Jeffrey."

He stared at his puzzled audience for a moment and smiled. "I was very lonely when I married my second wife. I had a young son who needed a mother. I was burning the candle at both ends trying to make a living and provide a home for Ted. I taught school all day and sold insurance at night. I was rarely home. I thought things would be better for Ted if I remarried."

Wilson stared sadly into the leaping flames in the fireplace. "I was sadly mistaken."

"What happened?" Adrienne's impetuous question surprised even her. She was so spellbound by what Wilson was saying, she didn't want him to stop. Kyle gave her fingers a reassuring squeeze.

"The marriage was doomed from the start, I'm afraid. We both married for all the wrong reasons. I don't think I really loved Angela—not the way I loved Ted's mother. But I was so desperate for a mother for Ted that I convinced myself that I did love her—in spite of what she was."

"What does that mean?" Jill's eyes were wide and she was sitting straight and tall in her chair. She'd been nibbling on the popcorn and sipping her hot chocolate at first, but now she was as enthralled with the unfolding story as Adrienne and Kyle.

"Too young, mostly. Young and irresponsible. At first that was what attracted me to her—her youthfulness, her zest for life." He gave a dry, humorless laugh. "I felt like all of that had been drained from me. My wife had died, I was left with a tiny child, my world had crumbled. I had no reasons left to be carefree."

Ted squirmed uncomfortably in his chair. It was obvious that he was familiar with this painful story his father seemed to be dragging from the very depths of his soul.

Wilson wiped a hand across his forehead and continued.

"Angela was little more than a child herself. I realize that now. She was running away from a bad situation at home as much as I was running away from the pain of Melissa's death. I was so charmed, so taken with her vivaciousness, her zest for life, that I didn't begin to think that once we were married, she'd still keep running."

Wilson's laugh was dry and bitter, crackling like the oak log on the fire. Adrienne jumped when a burning log broke in two and crumbled into the glowing ashes below the grate.

"I thought once we were married Angela would turn into Melissa—a homemaker, a wife, a mother. I expected her to cook and clean and take care of Ted and be satisfied and happy doing it."

"Wasn't she?" Jill's eyes reflected the dancing fire.

"Not a bit. She wanted someone to take care of her, someone to have fun with. She didn't want a child and a house and responsibility. She wanted to go dancing on Saturday nights. To go to movies, to travel. She wanted unlimited amounts of money so she could shop and buy the clothing and other things that she'd never had at home. I didn't find a mother for Ted . . ." Wilson's voice trailed away, "I found another child."

Ted picked up the story from his father. "Angela used to leave me home alone and go shopping or out for lunch with her friends. She said I was old enough to take care of myself."

"That started when Ted was barely seven." Wilson's voice held a tinge of anger.

"And when Jeffrey came, well . . ." Ted's voice took on a hurt, guarded tone.

"Once Jeffrey was born things went from bad to worse for Ted. Angela had never seemed to love Ted very much, but she'd never been really *bad* to him. But once Jeffrey arrived and she had a son that was her own, well . . ."

Adrienne's heart was aching so that she feared it might burst. No wonder Ted seemed suspicious and withdrawn!

"She didn't pay any attention to me at all then," Ted continued for his dad. "I had to do most of the chores around the house and cook my own breakfast. She wouldn't let me play with Jeffrey when she was around. The only time I was good enough for that was when she wanted to go out. Then I had to babysit."

Wilson tipped his head into his hands and gave a low, anguished moan. "And I let this go on!"

"It's not your fault, Dad. Please don't—"

"But it *is*. I was so wrapped up in making a living that I ignored how unhappy you were—how unhappy we *all* were. Even Jeffrey."

"Why Jeffrey?" It was the first time Kyle had spoken. He was staring at the sleeping child on Wilson's lap.

"Angela still hadn't grown up. When Jeffrey was a baby, he was cute and cuddly and she could pick him up when she wanted and give him to Ted or me when she was tired of him. Once he got older and developed a mind of his own, he wasn't as much fun for his mother." Wilson stared into the dying fire, his eyes glazed and dull. His next words were soft as a whisper. "We started having terrible fights."

Adrienne saw Ted wince at the memory. Her own parents rarely disagreed and their most heated arguments always ended with a smile and a hug. She could only imagine the kind of fighting Wilson and Ted were remembering.

"By the time Jeffrey was two, our marriage was a shambles and she left me."

Kyle and Adrienne exchanged a sorrowful glance. Adrienne nestled her fingers deeper into the palm of his hand. This crazy race through the woods to Wilson's cabin had uncorked a whole bottle of information that she'd never dreamed possible. Her insides felt cold and shivery and sad. Her own secure home seemed far away and unreal for a moment.

All the hateful, suspicious things she'd believed about Ed Wilson were disappearing like dew under the morning sun, but there were things she still did not understand.

"Where is she now?" Jill asked the question that was hovering in everyone's mind. "And why do you have Jeffr—"

The answer hit Adrienne with a jolt. "You took Jeffrey away from his mother! That's why you're hiding and that's why his picture was on the milk carton!"

Suddenly it all made sense. Ted resembled his father. Jeffrey resembled Wilson as well. Yet, the boys didn't really look like brothers at all. They were half-brothers, each carrying some of the traits of their mothers. But they were a family. A family that loved one another. Adrienne could tell that by the gentle, loving manner with which Wilson spoke of his sons.

And Jeffrey was curled trustingly against his father's chest, unaware of the storm brewing around him, assured that his father would take care of him.

"Then you *are* a kidnapper . . . sort of," Jill concluded. Adrienne cringed, wishing Jill would think before speaking.

"No! No, he's not! He saved Jeffrey! Angela was hurting him. My dad saved my brother!"

All eyes were on Ted. The boy was trembling and tears spilled down his cheeks. He clenched and unclenched his fists, struggling to regain control. Finally he sank back into his chair. "They could have hurt Jeffrey. They *would* have."

"Who?" The voices of Kyle, Jill and Adrienne chimed together.

A stormy shadow passed over Wilson's features. It was obvious that he didn't really want to discuss this horrible pain, but Adrienne sensed his need to explain.

"Angela started divorce proceedings against me. She moved about twenty miles from our house, so we didn't get to see Jeffrey very often. She didn't want us coming around, so we had to get a court order to see the child."

Adrienne stared at the little fellow snoring in Wilson's lap.

"Then what?"

"Jeffrey started to change." Ted said the words flatly, belying the emotion Adrienne sensed in them.

"Change? How?"

"He wouldn't play like he used to," Ted explained. "He got real quiet. And he said it hurt to run."

"We had Jeffrey with us so little that I didn't catch on at first," Wilson admitted. "All we had time for was to pick him up and take him out to eat at his favorite places . . ."

". . . or go to the zoo," Ted added.

"It wasn't until we took him swimming about two months ago that we discovered something was really wrong." Wilson and Ted were speaking quickly now, both eager to get the story over with.

"He had bruises all over his back and legs."

"When I asked Angela she said he'd fallen down the stairs."

"But Jeffrey told me he'd gotten spanked."

"And no child should get bruises like that from a spanking." Wilson's mouth was a grim line. "Angela and her new boyfriend were abusing Jeffrey."

"But can't you make them stop?" Adrienne gasped. "Go to the police? Something?"

"I told her I would." Wilson's anger flared at the memory. "She told me that if I reported them she would take Jeffrey away and I'd never see him again. She said she had all her plans in place and I couldn't stop her from leaving."

"Dad thinks she was planning to leave anyway and not tell him."

"Our finding out about the bruises would just make her leave that much sooner."

"After I talked to Angela, Jeffrey's bruises started getting worse."

"They were mad at Dad and taking it out on Jeffrey." Ted's voice cracked as a tear ran down his cheek. "Jeffrey started losing weight and he even got to be afraid of *me.*"

"We were desperate, Adrienne," Wilson turned pleading eyes toward her. "You can see why, can't you? We had to get Jeffrey away."

Adrienne's chest felt full and tight. It was difficult to breath. She wanted to cry.

"I saw your dad's ad in the paper and called him right away. This cabin sounded like exactly what I needed—private, remote, secluded. I made arrangements to tutor Ted before I took him out of school. That way, there wouldn't be any questions about his disappearance, at least. Then I asked for a semester off to do some studying of my own. I didn't want any loose ends that Angela could trace."

"Your name isn't really Wilson, is it?" Adrienne murmured.

"No." Wilson looked ashamed, sorrowful. "It's Conrad."

"That's why the kids looked so funny when we asked them their names," Adrienne reasoned. "Finally things are starting to make sense." It wasn't going to be easy thinking of him as Mr. Conrad now.

Mr. Wilson/Conrad's lips twitched. "As soon as we picked up Jeffrey we came up here, hoping for peace and quiet. Instead, we got a trail of visitors that didn't stop."

"Dad and his firewood."

"Your mother and her curtains."

"You and the extension cord."

"Everyone and their questions."

Adrienne hung her head. "I knew there was a mystery up here. I just wanted to solve it."

"Well, it wasn't a very pretty mystery, young lady. And now—"

Jill burst in on the conversation. "What about Jeffrey? Does he miss his mother?"

Jeffrey's father looked grim. "Jeffrey has never once asked for his mother or mentioned her name."

"Oh."

That said it all in Adrienne's mind. Poor Jeffrey. Poor Ted. Poor Mr . . .

"The mystery!" Adrienne blurted, her mind suddenly whirling.

"Us you mean?" Mr. Conrad sighed. "I think our family is more of a tragedy than a myst—"

"No! I didn't think you were a kidnapper when I started snooping around—" Adrienne dipped her head in embarrassment, "—investigating. I thought you were a *poacher*!"

"The poachers!" Ted, Kyle, Jill and Adrienne all jumped to their feet at once.

Mr. Conrad's eyes flew open. "What is going on?"

"We didn't tell you about the poachers!"

"You scared us 'cause we thought you were a kidnapper—"

"And you started to talk about Jeffrey—"

"And we didn't hear anyone following us—"

"So maybe they don't know where we went—"

"And then we got all wrapped up in your story, and—"

"Hold on!" Mr. Conrad held up both hands for silence, nearly waking the sleeping child on his lap. "What are you talking about?"

In a torrent of breathless words and broken phrases, they told of the poachers and Ted's part in freeing them.

"They were ugly and dirty and one had yellow teeth with junk all over them," Jill shuddered.

". . . dressed in camouflage clothes so they couldn't be seen in the forest," Kyle added.

"They were dressing out a deer. They've killed lots of animals today, the way they talked."

"I've been watching them all week, Dad. But I knew you didn't want anyone to find us, so I didn't say anything," Ted admitted.

"One was tall and skinny."

"And another one shorter and fatter."

"They were pretty old. The young one was about twenty-five."

"And I think he was the meanest," Jill assessed.

"They heard us when we tried to get away."

". . . and tied us up."

"We don't know what they were going to do with us after they'd loaded up their truck."

"But Ted came along and saved us!"

"You mean you kids just snuck to the cabin and came inside? Why didn't you tell me right away?"

Adrienne hung her head. "Because at first I

thought you were a poacher, too. And then, after I saw Jeffrey's picture on the milk carton, I thought you were a kidnapper." Her voice sounded low and far away. "I thought you'd hurt us, too."

"And then I started telling about Jeffrey . . . and it seemed so much safer and warmer in here with the fire going and the thick wooden doors . . . that you listened to my whole story." Conrad ran his fingers through his hair. "But now what are we going to do? Sounds to me like these men are dangerous. What if they come looking for you?"

"The clearing where they caught us is a long way from the cabin. Adrienne brought us here by a shortcut."

"I almost got lost doing it, too. The woods are really overgrown. We kept separating and then coming together. I don't think it would be very easy to follow our trail."

"Don't underestimate a criminal, Adrienne." It was Kyle, speaking from the window. He'd lifted a corner of the thick shade. In the silence after his comment, everyone could hear the crashing of running footsteps coming through the underbrush near the cabin.

The men's conversation was faint but understandable through the thick cabin walls.

"Do you think they got this far?"

"I dunno. What would they be doing up here?"

"I betcha they high-tailed it back to town."

"Yeh, and to the police."

"Let's knock on this door. Maybe they came here."

"Quick! You've got to hide." Conrad pushed the trio toward the bedroom. "Get under the bed. These guys have been here before. I recognize their voices. They told me they worked for the sheriff, watching the woods for poachers." He chuckled grimly. "Quite a cover, huh? Maybe they won't suspect I've got you in here."

Ted had lifted Jeffrey from his dad's arms. Now the older boy carried his brother to a cot near the fireplace. Quickly, he settled the child, then ran and climbed into the bed as Kyle, Jill and Adrienne crawled beneath it.

Conrad satisfied himself that none of the three could be seen beneath the bed's dust ruffle before he answered the pounding at the door.

"Who is it?" Conrad threw open the door on his unwelcome visitors.

"Howdy, Ed." Hank edged his way toward the door to glance inside the cabin.

"Hello. What can I do for you?"

Adrienne craned her neck. By squashing her cheek into the rough plank flooring, she could see beneath the dust ruffle. Ed's back was toward her. Hank and Carl's scruffy bodies filled the doorway.

"Your boy don't happen to be around, do he, Ed?" Hank spoke with studied casualness. No doubt Carl had told him what to say, Adrienne thought.

"Of course he is. Been here all day. We worked on his algebra and English studies until about a half hour ago. Ted laid down to take a nap while Jeffrey was sleeping." Ed tipped his head toward the bedroom.

Adrienne froze. Why was he doing that? Calling attention to the room and the very bed they were hiding under. Kyle's fingers found hers and he gave them a warm, reassuring squeeze.

Of course! Suddenly it made sense. Ted's father was just trying to act natural. By calling attention to the bedroom, he was probably diverting attention elsewhere. Adrienne heard Ted snuffle and roll across the bed.

"You sure he ain't been out? We saw some kids in

the woods and thought he might be with 'em." That was Carl's voice. It had a harsh, malicious ring.

"Kids? Up here? Not likely. Wish there were some around, though. Ted's been lonely, not being in school this month and all." Ed gave a laugh. "Guess he'll be glad to be back in the classroom after his nature trip in the backwoods."

"Kind of a crazy idea you had there, Wilson." Hank's voice still held a trace of disbelief.

"Dad?"

Adrienne felt the bed shudder as Ted rolled off the mattress. "Who's there, Dad?"

"It's no one for you, son. Go back to sleep."

Adrienne, looking through the bridge of Ted's bare feet so close to her she could have reached out and tickled him, saw Hank and Carl exchange glances.

"Well, I guess we'll be going." The two backed away from the door, apparently convinced of Ted and his father's charade.

Ted crawled back onto the bed, jiggling Adrienne's little peek hole.

"Bye, fellas. See you again."

"Mebbe, mebbe not," was the answer. The footsteps in the woods faded.

"Can we come out now?" Jill wailed. "I have dust up my nose and my hair is caught on a bedspring."

"Not yet. I want to make sure they're really gone. They wanted to catch up with you kids very badly in order to come and knock on my door."

"Pretty bold, too," Kyle commented. He was tucked awkwardly under the brace at the foot of the bed. He was much too big to be shoved into such a tiny space.

"Why?" Jill hissed.

"They've been to the cabin before. Don't they think they're ever going to get caught?"

"Dumb, not bold, that's what they are. But I'd bet

you money they'll be a hundred miles away from here by nightfall."

"No!" Adrienne scrambled out from beneath the bed. "We can't let them get away!"

Jill and Kyle followed close on her heels. "We've got to report them! You've got a jeep. We can take the back road down to our farm and call the police from there. If we hurry, they won't get far."

"I'm afraid I'll have to say 'no' this time, Adrienne."

Ed Conrad's tone stopped her cold. Adrienne turned to stare at him with bewildered eyes.

He was obviously very upset.

"Sir? What's wrong?"

"I can't take you down and march you into the sheriff's office. Have you forgotten? I'm a fugitive, too. If I do that, I'll lose Jeffrey—and perhaps Ted."

A sick feeling lodged in Adrienne's stomach.

"I was a fool to spirit them away, but now I've made my choice. We'll have to keep running. At first, all I wanted was to get Jeffrey away, to protect him. Maybe all I've done is make his life as much of a nightmare as it was before. I don't want to run, but I will. I'll do anything to keep my sons."

Adrienne, forthright as usual, burst out with the thought that had been running through her mind.

"Don't run. Turn yourself in."

"What?"

"No!" Ted cried. "Don't listen to her, Dad!"

"I'm not all that smart," Adrienne continued, "but it seems to me, that you had pretty good reasons for taking Jeffrey away. That doesn't make it *right*, exactly, but nothing will make it right again except taking him back and fighting for him the right way."

Ed stared at Adrienne until she wondered if her red hair had ignited and was burning.

"When I do things that are bad or wrong or stupid, things that hurt people even though I don't mean to hurt anyone, I always pray about it." Adrienne talked with great feeling, desperately wanting Ed to understand. "First I ask God to forgive me for what I've done. Next I try to undo some of the damage. Sometimes I have to apologize and ask someone else's forgiveness." She grinned. "It's easier to ask for God's forgiveness, though. You can always count on Him to forgive you."

"I think Adrienne's right, sir," Kyle stepped forward and put his hands on Adrienne's shoulders. "You and Ted and Jeffrey can't live like this forever. This isn't a real life. If you don't go back and try to straighten things out, you'll never be happy. You'll always be worrying about getting caught."

"Anyway," Jill concluded, "your wife, Angela, doesn't sound like a very nice lady. Why would they believe her when your sons say they love you?"

"Why, indeed?" Ed asked softly, as though what the three were saying had never occurred to him before.

"The woods aren't safe with the poachers loose," Adrienne pointed out. "And," her eyes brightened, "maybe we could put in a good word for you. Would anyone believe us?" Her hopeful gaze bore into Ed's tortured face.

Ed turned and stared into the dying fire. "I don't know if anyone else would, but *I'm* beginning to. . . ."

No one dared to disturb him. Silently, Ted began to heat milk on the tiny gas stove. Jill and Adrienne measured cocoa into clean mugs. Kyle put new logs on the fire.

They were all sitting in a semi-circle, staring into the blaze when Jeffrey awoke.

"Chocolate for Jeffrey?" he asked, stretching and yawning like a newly awakened puppy.

"I'll make you some. Just a minute." Ted jumped to his feet.

He rummaged for a minute in the cupboard.

"Sorry, Jeffrey, old boy, we seem to be out of cocoa. And we're on our last box of powdered milk." Ted's head disappeared under the counter. He reappeared with a nearly empty bag of Oreos. "We're down to the last three of your favorite cookies, too. Guess we're going to have to find a way to go shopping."

"That won't be necessary."

Ed Wilson/Conrad had been silent so long that when he spoke everyone jumped.

"We can't go much longer with these supplies, Dad. Tuna fish, peanut butter, we're running out of everything."

Ed turned toward his son. "We're going to be leaving this place. I've thought about it. Your friends are right. I can't ignore the information I have about the poachers any longer. And I can't ask you and Jeffrey to live like two little fugitives from justice. I'll take you all to town. We can tell them everything we know about that miserable trio in the woods." Ed paused, "And I can turn myself in."

Chapter Ten

Ted was crying. Jeffrey set up a wail simply because he'd never seen his big brother cry before and it frightened him. Jill sat near the fire, shedding a few tears of her own.

Kyle walked with Ted to the far side of the room, murmuring something in the boy's ear that Adrienne could not hear. She picked up Jeffrey and walked over to Ed Conrad.

"Sir, I think you're doing the right thing," Adrienne spoke softly. Jeffrey snuffled near her ear.

"For one so young, you certainly are clear on what's right and wrong."

"Yessir. My dad talks about things like that alot. He talks about what it says in the Bible about the way we should live. He thinks it's very important, and I guess I do, too. He and my mom teach me a lot just by the way *they* live."

Ed shook his head and sat down. "I wish I'd been as smart as you, Adrienne. Now I've gone and ruined everything for my family."

"Maybe not. You don't know that."

"Even if the law can forgive what I've done, I can't forgive myself." He ran shaking fingers through the coarse strands of his hair.

"What about God?" Jeffrey quit crying and Adrienne set him on the floor to run to his older brother. She placed her hands on her hips and stared at the top of Ed's head until he lifted it to meet her gaze.

"What about Him?"

"You can ask His forgiveness. He *always* forgives us if we are really and truly sorry for what we've done and give up whatever bad thing it is. Jesus didn't just come to earth to be a good example for us. He came to be the complete sacrifice for our sins—if we'll believe in Him. My dad says that's the forgiving that counts. And anyway, if God can forgive you—and He's perfect—you should be able to forgive yourself."

Conrad slapped his open palms on his legs. "You make an awful lot of sense for a kid, Adrienne Fuller."

Adrienne grinned. "My dad says that most of the time I don't make any sense at all—especially my taste in clothes."

Conrad chuckled at first. Then he tilted his head back and gave a full-blown roaring laugh.

"Wowee!" he pronounced when he was through. "That's the first time in months I've felt free enough to laugh. It felt wonderful. Thanks, Adrienne."

Adrienne ducked her head. She didn't want any thanks. All she wanted was for Ed, Jeffrey and Ted to be a real family—without any secrets to hide—once again.

It was a silent ride into town. Ed had insisted on packing up their belongings at the cabin and putting them on the luggage rack of the jeep. "Easier," he said, "for whatever comes next."

They'd stopped at the Fuller house to pick up Adrienne's father.

"You're dad's in town, Adrienne," Naomi announced, wiping her hands on the corner of her apron and staring curiously into the jeep packed with luggage and people.

"Will you call him, Mom? Ask him to meet us at the police station. And have him get the game warden, too. We've seen the poachers." Adrienne chose not to go into the facts of Ted and his father. That would take an entire evening to explain.

Naomi nodded briskly. Adrienne had to give her mother credit. She might be a worrier sometimes, but when things needed to be done, Naomi didn't get frantic and ask a lot of questions.

Adrienne felt like a concrete block or a big stone was sitting in the middle of her chest, cutting off her breathing. It was because of Ted and Jeffrey, she knew. She'd watched them cling to their father as they packed at the cabin and now as they waited in the jeep.

Ted clung because he didn't know what would happen next. Jeffrey only sensed the sadness and tension in the ones he loved and responded the best way he knew how.

Ted continued to stay close by his dad at the police station.

Wayne Fuller was already there. So was the game warden, drinking coffee and propping his feet up on an old brass spittoon.

"Adrienne, your mother said I should meet you here." Wayne stood up quickly and eyed his daughter.

Adrienne waved a hand. "Don't worry, I'm fine, Dad. We just had a little run-in with the poachers."

"What?" the uniformed man came to his feet in a single, fluid motion. "What did you just say?"

"The poachers. We ran into them in a clearing in the woods."

"Did you get a good look?"

Adrienne, Kyle and Jill glanced at each other. "Too good."

"It was horrible, sir. They tied us up and if Ted hadn't come with his knife and . . ." Jill had been silent for so long, Adrienne had almost forgotten her friend. When the torrent of words and tears began to flow from her, it surprised them all.

"Hold up, there, little lady. Who tied you up? And where'd this knife come from?" The sheriff, the game warden and Wayne Fuller were all on their feet now. It was going to take a long time to unshuffle the facts and lay them straight.

Nearly an hour had passed by the time each of the four teenagers had told their stories. Ted's version was short and to the point. Adrienne knew that every word cost him a great deal, for he knew what was coming next.

Jill's rendition was embellished with the dramatic flair that came so naturally to her. Kyle's story was clear and to the point. Adrienne smiled to herself. All those brains gave him good organizational abilities. She told her own version of the story as best she could, leaving out the fact that it was really Mr. Wilson/Conrad she'd suspected of poaching.

The game warden had left and the sheriff was already on the wire calling for more assistance when Adrienne's small voice broke into the hubbub. "There's more, sir."

"More? What more could you kids have gotten yourselves into in one afternoon?" The sheriff stared at them. Adrienne could feel her father's eyes boring into her back.

"I'd like to turn myself in." Ed Conrad stood. Ted started to weep.

"What in the world for? You been poaching, too?" The sheriff began scratching the top of his head with the end of his pencil.

"No. But I've done something which you might think is even worse."

Kyle's fingers curled around Adrienne's. They were warm and strong and comforting. Adrienne closed her eyes, as if to shut out what was about to happen.

"I think you'd better explain." The sheriff's voice was suddenly cold and hard. Wayne Fuller settled himself into the chair once again.

Ed told his story unevenly and nervously, much like he'd told it back at the cabin. Before he'd finished, Ted had moved his chair next to his father's and Jeffrey had crawled onto his lap.

Jeffrey, unable to understand what his father was saying, busied himself tracing the lines and creases of his father's face with a chubby index finger.

To look at them, they made a perfect family picture. But in this case, seeing was not everything.

"And that's about it," Ed concluded. "I didn't want to lose Jeffrey and I didn't want him hurt anymore. So I took him. It was wrong. I regret ever having done it." A weary smile washed across his features. "But Adrienne, here, gave me a lecture about right and wrong . . . and about forgiveness. I don't know if the law can forgive me, but she told me about Someone who can." His laugh was gentle. "I'd nearly forgotten about God in the mess I've made of my life. We were friends once. I think we can be again."

The sheriff looked as though he could have been knocked off his chair with a feather. Adrienne resisted the impulse to go and give him a poke with her finger just to see if he really would tumble off the chair and roll across the floor. Her father was no less amazed.

"Well, Mr., er, Wilson . . ." the sheriff began.

"The name is Conrad. Ed Conrad. It will be nice to go back to using my own name, at least. I've missed it." Ed mused. "Dishonesty doesn't suit me very well."

"But you have taken the law into your own hands," the sheriff began. "No doubt there's been a warrant issued for your arrest. There's a judge waiting to see you."

"I imagine so. Angela, no matter how little she really cared for Jeffrey, wouldn't let me go unpunished."

"I'm afraid I'll have to take you into custody." The sheriff stood.

"Then what will happen to him?" Adrienne blurted. Now that it was really happening, it seemed so scary. She'd had enough bad scares for one day.

"That's up to the judge, little lady. Depends on how kindly he takes to fathers who spirit away their own children."

"But what about Ted and Jeffrey? What will happen to them?"

"Since his mother isn't living, Ted will probably be sent to a foster home while this thing is being sorted out."

The moan that Ted gave sent shivers down Adrienne's spine. Ed sank lower in his chair.

The sheriff continued. "And the little guy, well, I suppose he'll be sent back to his mother."

"No! No go!" It was Jeffrey this time. He'd stopped some minutes earlier running his palms across his father's cheeks, Adrienne had noticed. Apparently he'd understood that this conversation involved *him*. "Want Daddy."

Even the sheriff's eyes misted over the toddler's simple statement. Weakly, he reached for the phone. "I think I'd better call County Social Services to handle this," he murmured. His hand was trembling at the dial.

Wayne Fuller stood up. "We have to go, kids. This family needs to be alone together now." He laid his hand on Ed's shoulder. "We'll pray for you."

Ed nodded. "We need it."

Silently Wayne marshalled the three teenagers onto the street.

"I think I want to go home now." Jill's voice

sounded tinny and faraway. She looked like she was about to be ill.

"I'll take you home first," Wayne stated. "And I want you to take a bath and crawl into bed as soon as you've told your parents what happened. You look like you're about to faint."

"If I was going to faint, I should have done it earlier," Jill reasoned. "Now nothing is happening and my knees are shaking and . . ."

"Delayed response," Kyle pointed out. "Very common in cases of—"

"Oh, be quiet," Jill huffed. "I think a lecture now might be worse than facing the poachers."

Kyle grinned good-naturedly. "Well, if nothing else, you two girls have broken me of my habit of using big words. My dad even asked me what was wrong the other day when I asked for a spoon instead of a serving utensil." In spite of her distress, Adrienne had to smile. A lot of things had happened in such a short while.

Once Jill was deposited at the Wainright's, Wayne Fuller turned his vehicle toward home.

"You've got a car at our place, don't you, Kyle?"

"Yessir. Didn't know I'd be here quite so long."

"I can imagine. Whatever possessed you kids to go traipsing through the woods like that, anyway? I thought you were smart enough to know better or I would have forbidden it entirely."

"It's my fault, Dad. I wanted to investigate."

"I should have known."

"I thought Mr. Wilson—Mr. Conrad—was the poacher. I knew they were acting funny, I just didn't know the real reason."

"I'm considering tying you to the bedpost until you're ready to graduate from high school, Adrienne. Would that keep you in line?" Mr. Fuller breathed his exasperated response.

"I doubt it," Kyle and Adrienne chimed together. Laughter filled the vehicle.

It feels good to laugh, Adrienne thought. She wondered when Ted and Jeffrey would be able to laugh again.

"Dad?"

"Yes, Adrienne."

"When will we find out what's going to happen to Ted and Jeffrey and their father?"

"I'll check with the sheriff in a couple of days. Until then I want you two to stay out of trouble."

"No investigating?"

"None at all."

"Not even a little bit?"

"What do you have in mind, Adrienne?"

"I still don't know what happened to PorkChop. I really didn't have time to go into it until now. Maybe I could 'wind down' by finding out who stole him."

"Does that sound safe enough to you, Kyle?" Wayne asked.

"Safer than kidnappers and poachers."

"These guys are only porknappers," Adrienne offered.

"Porknappers!" Wayne and Kyle bellowed together.

"I *am* going to chain her to the bedpost," Wayne joked.

"Securely, I hope," Kyle joined in.

All three were laughing when they turned into the Fuller yard some miles down the road.

Kyle was whistling when Adrienne met him in the hallway the next morning.

"What's with you?" she teased.

"So your dad unchained you for school, huh?"

"Just barely. I haven't had a lecture like that one since I accidently left the pasture gate open and all the cattle escaped."

"You probably deserved it."

"Probably," Adrienne agreed. She was feeling better this morning. There would be no more poachers in the woods. If only she could feel good about Ted and his family, it would be a perfect day. Obviously Kyle was happy too.

"So, what's the whistling about?" she asked.

He shrugged as he turned toward his locker. "Yesterday made me do some pretty serious thinking."

"It was a pretty serious day."

"My parents were worried by the time I got home."

"And?"

"I told them where I'd been and what had happened."

"What did they say?"

"It's not really what *they* said that made me happy," Kyle mused. "It's more what *I* was finally able to say to them."

"What do you mean?"

"I thought about Ted and Jeffrey and how much their dad loved them and how far he'd go to try and keep them with him."

"But it was wrong, Kyle. Illegal."

"I know that. But if he'd go that far for his sons, I decided to tell my parents that they could go a little ways, at least, for me."

"What did you ask them to do?" Adrienne breathed.

"I asked them to start coming to church—with me—as a family."

"You did?" Adrienne's eyes were round. "What did they say?"

"At first they didn't like it. They said all the usual things about hocus-pocus and gobbledy-gook."

"Then what?"

Then they said they'd try it—once."

"Just once?"

"And I said they had to give it six months."

"Wow! What did they say then?"

"That was too long."

"And you said . . ." Adrienne was impressed with Kyle's determination.

"I said it really wasn't long enough. And, you know what? They agreed!"

Unthinkingly, Adrienne dropped her books in the middle of the hallway, wrapped her arms around Kyle's waist and gave a loud whoop of delight. As soon as she'd done it, she realized what a scene she'd caused. She glanced anxiously at Kyle's face.

He was smiling.

"Look at those two. 'Mr. Brain' and 'Miss I'm-Going-to-be-a-Doctor.' Don't they *ever* give up?"

The voice came from the far side of the corridor. Two senior boys were eyeing them—Rory Olson and Mike Wills. Adrienne didn't particularly like either of them. They were mean to the underclassmen and always bragging about how great they were. And she remembered how pleased they'd looked the day Melvin had escaped.

Kyle whispered in Adrienne's ear. "Ignore them. They're just troublemakers. Come on. We'll be late for class."

Adrienne gave the pair a long, cold stare. What had they just said? "Don't they ever give up?" What in the world was that supposed to mean?

Her thoughts were diverted for the rest of the day by an advanced algebra test last hour. After school, she met Jill and Kyle at the schoolbus.

"What's up?" Kyle asked casually, then looking into Adrienne's eyes, added, "or shouldn't I ask?"

Adrienne sank into the seat next to his, thoughtfully chewing her lip. "Something funny is going on."

"Oh, no, you don't!" Jill protested, waving her hands in front of her face. "This is where I came in last time. I got tied up, scared out of my wits, almost *murdered*, ruined a perfectly good sweatshirt—"

"This is not the same thing, Jill," Adrienne gave her friend a disgusted glance. "I think I have a lead on who stole PorkChop."

That was all it took to get Jill interested. "Who?"

"Remember those two senior guys who were making fun of us in the hall this morning, Kyle?"

"I told you not to pay attention to them, Adrienne. They just like to make trouble."

"That's what I mean. Remember, one of them said, 'Don't they *ever* give up?' Remember?"

"Yeh. So what?"

"I think they mean don't we ever give up liking science, wanting to be a doctor, or *giving up on a project once it looks like it's been ruined.*"

Kyle's eyes looked a little brighter. "Do you think that's possible?"

"Sure I do. The way they said it made it sound like wanting to do well in school was *bad*. I'll bet they thought it would be funny to see Jill and me try to make a show at the junior/senior fair and fall on our faces."

"Just like it would be funny to let Melvin out of his cage and scare the whole school."

"Or set all the tables in the cafeteria so the cooks would have to unset them before lunch."

"*Or* hang all the bulletin boards upside down."

"Could be."

"Maybe you've got a point."

"I'm sure I do," Adrienne crowed. Then the light in her eyes faded. "But what can I do about it? We don't have any proof."

Jill snapped her fingers. "We've got to *trick* them into being caught." Her eyes danced. "This should be easy, after the poachers."

Adrienne ran her fingers through her spikey red hair. "Easy, huh? Well, I don't know about that. . . ."

Adrienne's hunch was correct. It wasn't as easy as Jill had thought. She'd been watching the pair—Rory Olson and Mike Wills—for two days. They were up to something, but she couldn't tell what. It all stemmed from a conversation she'd overheard in the lunchroom. Adrienne had been carrying her tray toward Jill's table while Rory and Mike were emptying their dirty utensils onto the conveyor that carried the used trays back to the kitchen.

"Hey, Wills, you got the . . . stuff?"

"Of course. Don't worry about it."

"We don't want anything to go wrong."

"It won't. Hasn't before."

"Yeh, well, we were lucky. Maybe we should . . . you know. Quit."

"Now? Come off it, Wills. Just once more. Just 'cause you didn't like handling, well, never mind. We're *seniors*. We've got to make our mark on the school—just so people remember the class. Why . . . it's like our *duty*."

She was mulling it over again in her mind when Kyle approached. "Hi."

Adrienne gave him a slow, delighted smile. There was a special bond of friendship between them now. Just seeing him brightened her day.

"What's new?" she inquired.

"I'm not sure." He looked puzzled.

"What's that supposed to mean?"

"I just saw something funny in the back of Rory Olson's car."

"What? A clue?"

"I don't think so. Just a lot of paint cans. Used ones. Some had colors dripping down the sides—red, blue—nothing that matched."

"So maybe his folks are going to paint their house." Paint cans didn't sound like much of a clue to the pair's next prank.

"I thought of that, but the Olsons just moved into a new house about six months ago. I don't think they'd be painting yet—at least not with those bright colors."

"Bright? Really bright?"

"Yeh. Ugly, too. Wonder what it's for?"

The two of them were sitting side by side on the bottom bleacher when Jill came prancing toward them. "You two look confused," she announced cheerfully.

"We are. We're trying to figure out what prank Olson and Wills are going to pull next. At least," and Adrienne paused, "I *think* it's Olson and Wills."

"Oh, them," Jill waved Adrienne's comment aside with a brush of her hand. "They're too weird for words. I saw them this morning trying to pick the lock on the door to the girls' locker room." Jill turned up her nose. "Sleaze-bags."

Kyle and Adrienne turned and stared at one another. It was as though the same idea had struck both minds at once.

"The paint cans!"

"What? What? What paint cans?" Jill piped, not wanting to be left out.

"What a way to 'make a mark on the school.' "

"Those creeps."

"And everybody will get in trouble if they don't get caught."

"Tell me what you're talking about!" Jill screeched, causing her voice to echo off the gym walls.

"We think Rory and Mike are going to use some ugly paint that Kyle saw in the back of Rory's car to paint the girls' locker room."

"Adrienne heard them talking about 'making their mark' on the school before they left. You saw them trying to pick the lock."

"And, anyway," Adrienne concluded, "the girls'

locker room is only concrete cinder blocks anyway. They wouldn't dare put it on good walls. It's just like them to think this is funny."

"Maybe that little cracker box of a room needs paint," Jill pointed out. "You can hardly turn around in there. The boys got the big room and we got a closet. It's got low ceilings and it's stuffy and smelly and creepy—"

"That's it! That's it!" Adrienne snapped her fingers. "You've just given me an idea!"

"What?"

"For once, Rory Olson and Mike Wills are going to have one of their pranks backfire on them."

Kyle and Jill stared at Adrienne as she concluded, "And all we're going to need is Mr. Palley's help."

Eleven

"How can you be sure they're going to do it to-night?" Jill wondered as they prepared to catch Rory and Mike in the act of painting the girls' locker room.

"Because it's the only night of the week that there isn't basketball practice or cheerleading practice or something else going on in the gym. Besides, most of the teachers are in the elementary rooms for the in-service training classes. It's perfect."

"Are you sure Rory and Mike are smart enough to think of all this?" Jill wondered skeptically.

Adrienne grinned. "I forgot to mention that Kyle managed to overhear Mike and Rory bragging about the next big trick that was coming up. They said that Friday morning the whole school would know."

"Sounds like this is the night, then. How'd you get Mr. Palley to go along with this?"

"He said I was one of his best students. If I couldn't borrow some 'equipment' from the science lab, no one could. Anyway, he thought the idea was kind of funny. He kept saying 'turnabout is fair play.' And anyway, if Rory and Mike don't do anything wrong, nothing will happen."

"Adults are even stranger than kids, sometimes," Jill commented. "Let's get going."

It was easy to turn up the heat in the girls' locker room. The control was located just outside the door, in the corridor, next to the light switch.

Jill busied herself removing the door handle from the inside of the door.

Kyle unscrewed the unexposed light bulbs in the ceiling and stuffed the heat vents leading from the room while Adrienne deposited the science room "equipment" in the room. Then they both backed slowly out leaving the door slightly ajar.

"I didn't know you could sit up here," Jill exclaimed, swinging her legs over the rafters that covered the gymnasium stage. "You can see out over the gymnasium or down into the corridor where the locker rooms are . . ."

". . . without being seen," Adrienne finished. "I found out about it when I worked props for the class play."

"Shhhhh. I hear footsteps!"

"Teachers?"

"No. They aren't going to be done for two hours yet. I think it's Rory and Mike."

The three silently watched from their bird's-eye perch as Rory Olson and Mike Wilson made their way to the locker room door. Their whispers carried to the far reaches of the rafters.

"The door's open!"

"Better yet. Let's get inside. This paint is heavy."

"Close the door before someone comes. There's a light switch on the far wall."

From where they were, the trio could hear the door latch slip into place.

Quickly, Adrienne, Kyle and Jill made their way down a ladder to the stage floor. They hurried to the closed locker room door to listen to the conversation inside.

"These lights aren't coming on! Can you find another switch?"

"There's one outside the door. Just let me make my way—"

"It sure is hot in here. Feels like a hundred degrees."

"Hey! This door is stuck!"

"Stuck? It can't be—"

A crash echoed in the little room.

"What was that?"

"I just stepped in this dumb paint bucket. I've got paint all over. Find the light!"

There was a violent wrenching and tugging on the doorhandle.

"It won't open, Rory. Rory?"

"Mike, there's something in here with us."

"Sure. All that paint you dumped on the floor."

"No. I mean *something*. Some *thing*. It touched me."

"Nah. It's the paint cans. I—hey! It just touched me!"

"We gotta get out of here!"

Adrienne nudged Kyle in the ribs. "Quick, go get Mr. Palley."

Kyle took off full speed for the elementary rooms. The noise inside the locker room was getting louder. The knob shaking had turned into full-fledged door pounding by the time Kyle and Mr. Palley arrived.

Mr. Palley pulled a glittering silver key from his ever-present lab coat. Theatrically, he slipped it into the lock and turned it.

The door swung open. Rory Olson stood, blinking at the sudden bright light, his feet and hands bathed in red paint. To his left was Mike Wills—with Melvin draped cozily about his legs.

"So these are the boys who have been playing all the pranks!" Mr. Palley announced. "Good for you,

Melvin, you found them!" Palley leaned over, picked up the snake and handed it to Adrienne.

"Here Adrienne, would you please put Melvin back into his cage? I've moved the cage next to the cooler. You know which cooler, of course, the one from which your science display, *PorkChop*, disappeared." Rory and Mike hung their heads guiltily.

Palley winked at them as Adrienne and her friends hurried Melvin back to his home.

Outside the school after Jill had left, Kyle stopped Adrienne. "We're a pretty good investigating team, Fuller."

"Not bad at all, Rogers." Adrienne's eyes twinkled. "I think Mr. Palley enjoyed that little trick."

"I hope Mike and Rory enjoy cleaning up all that paint they spilled . . ."

". . . and explaining why they were in that room, anyway."

"I think we've seen the end of the pranks around Hartwell High."

"Yeh," Adrienne sighed.

"What's wrong? You sound disappointed."

"It's just that now that we're sure who stole PorkChop, I haven't got that to think about anymore. All that's left to think about is . . ."

"Ted and Jeffrey?"

"And their dad."

Kyle nodded somberly. Then, sliding quickly from one mood to another, Adrienne announced, "Maybe my dad has heard something! He was going to try to find out what was happening to Ted and Jeffrey. If he's home, he might have some news for us."

Kyle and Adrienne raced to the Roger's car. PorkChop was avenged. Once again they were intent on the fate of the Rogers family.

Wayne Fuller was loading cleaning supplies into

the trunk of his car when Kyle and Adrienne arrived.

"Hi, there. I was just about to call the school and find out where you two were. I thought when you called and said you'd be getting a ride home with Kyle, you'd come right away."

Adrienne and Kyle exchanged glances.

"Sorry, sir. We came as soon as we could."

"Kyle and I helped Mr. Palley find the people who stole PorkChop, Dad." Adrienne's eyes began to sparkle. "It was great. We've been investigating all week. When Kyle heard these guys say that the whole school would find out about their next big trick on Friday, why we—"

"A regular Sherlock Holmes, that's what you've become, Adrienne," her father interjected. He glanced at his watch. "But right now we have to get going. I'd planned to be at the cabin by now."

Adrienne was surprised. Normally her father had plenty of time to hear how her day at school had been. She was especially disappointed with his abruptness today when she wanted to tell him about locating the pranksters who had been tormenting the students and staff all fall. What was so important up at the cabin?

"How come we have to go up to the cabin now, Dad?"

"Your mother wants her cleaning supplies up there. Now that we've lost our renters, she's decided to clean it up and see if it can be rented again this fall. That is," and Wayne paused to study Adrienne, "Unless you think you have enough money for college already in the bank."

"No, sir!" Adrienne headed for the car door.

As she turned back to wave goodbye to Kyle, her father inquired, "Coming, Kyle? I'd like to have you join us."

"You would?" Kyle looked as surprised as Ad-

rienne felt. Her father was acting very strangely today—excited, in his own mild sort of way. Adrienne
scratched her head.

"What's going on, Daddy?"

Mr. Fuller shot her a sideways glance. "Why should
anything be going on?"

"It just seems to me—"

"Well, it seems to me, young lady, that this sleuthing has gone to your head. If I can't invite Kyle to
the cabin without having you troubling me with questions, why, then you'd better just quit reading a mystery into everything I do or say."

Adrienne sank deep into the seat and rolled her
eyes. Now she was *sure* something was wrong with
her father. She wished she knew what it was.

She sat between Kyle and her father on the bumpy
trip to the cabin. The rutted road made the car creak
and shimmy as they wound their way through the
forest.

Kyle's broad shoulder brushed hers as he leaned
to whisper in her ear. "What's going on?"

"Got me."

Their questions began to be answered as they
neared the clearing. A familiar vehicle sat in front of
the open door to the cabin.

"Is that Mr. Conrad's?" Adrienne wondered aloud.

"Same license plate," Kyle noted.

They both turned to stare at Wayne Fuller. His lip
was twitching with suppressed delight.

"They're here? Now?" Adrienne sat bolt upright in
the seat and peered through the windshield.

Her father's smile broadened.

When the car rolled to a stop, Kyle and Adrienne
scrambled out, tripping on each other's feet. Before
they could go any farther, Jeffrey came shooting from
around the far edge of the jeep to clamp his arms
around Adrienne's legs.

Adrienne's eyes were watery as she knelt to pick up the little boy.

"Hi! I never thought you'd get here!" It was Ted. His father followed close behind.

Kyle and Adrienne exchanged astounded looks. Why were they all here? And how?

Ed saw the question in their eyes and decided it was time to explain.

"We've come to pick up some of our things," he chuckled. "I guess we didn't pack so well when we left the first time. I suppose there was too much excitement going on."

"But . . . you're together!" Adrienne blurted. "I thought—"

"Come on inside, all of you. I think I've got a lot to tell." Ed led the way into the cabin that was now so familiar to all of them. Adrienne and Kyle sank onto the couch while Wayne took a straightbacked chair. Ted and Jeffrey curled together on the rug while Mr. Conrad paced the floor.

"I suppose you're wondering how we managed to get back here."

"You aren't—"

"On the run? No, not anymore." Ed looked somber. "I learned the hard way how dangerous it is to take the law into your own hands. When we returned to Minneapolis, I was taken before the judge who'd issued the warrant for my arrest. It was up to him what happened next."

"And?"

"First of all, I was fined for being in contempt of court," Ed dipped his head. "Never thought an upstanding citizen like myself would be in such a predicament. Anyway," he continued, "that judge had to decide what to do with me."

Ed shuddered. "What he did was to scare me half out of my mind. Once I was sure I'd never see my boys or the outside of a prison again, he told me that since I had no other criminal record—not even a parking ticket or an overdue bill—that he'd sentence me to sixty days in jail and a fine."

"But it hasn't been sixty days since you turned yourself in!"

"No. He suspended the jail sentence if, in the future, I break no laws and abide within the orders of the court. If I don't do that, I go to jail. And," Ed added, "I do have to pay the fine."

"That doesn't seem so bad," Kyle commented. "I thought it would be worse."

"A couple of things worked in my favor," Ed went on. First, I had no criminal record, and second, Angela left the state without pressing charges. Apparently she decided that life was easier without any of us. Once she'd gotten over being angry with me for taking the child, she realized she was free again—and liked it."

Adrienne's gaze fell on Jeffrey. He was curled contentedly in Ted's arms. She couldn't imagine someone not wanting that little guy, but there were all kinds of people in the world. And Jeffrey was lucky to have been given a father and brother that loved him so much.

"I've done a terrible thing," Ed murmured. "I've had a good deal of trouble forgiving myself for the stupidity and actual sinfulness of my actions." His voice crackled with emotion. "But I've been given a second chance. I'm not going to make a mess of it this time. Adrienne helped me see that."

"I did?" She was dumbfounded. How had she helped? She'd been afraid ever since the night they had gone to the sheriff that she'd helped to ruin their lives forever. "How?"

"I've been thinking about what you said that night in the cabin. About turning things over to God. When

I gave myself up to the authorities, I turned everything else in my life over to God." He paused to stare
out the window that was finally open and free of shut-
tering curtains. "I'd hung on to my problems for so
long that it was difficult to let them go. But I realized
that I hadn't done a very good job of solving them by
myself. I knew I needed help. He seemed to be the only
one left to turn to."

"And is He helping you now?"

"Every step of the way. When I finally put my mud-
dled up life in His hands . . . well, you know what?"

"No. What?" Adrienne's eyes were large with anticipation.

"Life has been better for me than ever before. I've
been frightened, I've been worried about what's going
to happen to the boys, all those things. But I've also
felt reassured that it will all work out for the best. And
it *is* working out, isn't it boys?"

Ted and Jeffrey nodded together.

Adrienne felt Kyle's fingers find hers across the
cushions of the couch. If she got any happier, Adrienne thought as she stared around the room at
these people she'd grown to love, she was afraid her
heart would burst.

Just when she thought she was going to have to
breakdown and blubber like a baby from sheer joy,
her father slapped his hands against his thighs and
stood up.

"And now—much as I hate to break up this party—
Kyle, Adrienne and I have one more stop to make tonight."

There was more? Adrienne didn't think she could
handle any more tonight. She was thankful for Kyle's
silent, undemanding presence by her side because
her father seemed bent on jerking her through a
whole series of surprises.

Their goodbyes were a tearful combination of

"thank-yous" and "let's keep in touch." As the Fuller car pulled away from the cabin, Ted, Jeffrey and Ed stood in the doorway, waving and smiling.

As the figures in the doorway dimmed and disappeared, Adrienne laid her head against the seat. "I can't take many more surprises like this, Dad. Why didn't you warn us?"

"You know, Adrienne Fuller, that no one—absolutely *no one*—likes a surprise better than you."

"I used to, Dad. I think I've been all surprised-out for the time being."

"Just one more. I think you and Kyle will like this one too."

Soon her father was pulling up in front of the sheriff's office.

"What are we doing here?" she blurted.

"Look, there's Wainright's car. Is Jill here too?" Kyle was as puzzled as she.

The pair trailed Fuller into the station.

A photographer from the daily paper was there waiting, along with the sheriff, the game warden and two men Adrienne recognized as reporters.

"Isn't it great news?" Jill shot toward them. "And we helped!"

"What? What?" Adrienne's head was spinning.

"They caught the poachers, silly! Didn't your dad tell you? And we're getting credit for helping to crack the poaching ring in Hartwell county. We're going to have our pictures in the newspaper and everything."

Before Adrienne and Kyle had time to consider the honor they were about to receive, the photographer was pushing them into place. The game warden and the sheriff shook hands with each of them while the camera flashed and the reporters asked questions.

A tingle of excitement played on Adrienne's spine. Now *this* was exciting. *This* was what life should be like. Her grin widened. She saw her father wink at her from the corner of her eye. The photographer's lens caught her winking back.

Behind her back, where no one—not her father or the man with the persistently flashing camera could see—Kyle's large, warm hand enveloped her own tiny one in a gentle squeeze.

Kyle.

How could she have ever thought he was boring?

Then again, Adrienne mused, she'd seen and done and learned a lot about herself and others in the past few weeks—things she'd never before even imagined. One thing she'd learned was that her mother was right.

Life was never boring with Adrienne Fuller around.